D1453551

Selected novels by Demetrio Aguilera-Malta...

Jaguar
Requiem for the Devil
Seven Moons and Seven Serpents
The General's Been Kidnapped
The Virgin Island
Madrid
Canal Zone

don goyo

CONTEMPORARY LITERATURE

don goyo, Demetrio Aguilera-Malta, *1980*

don goyo

By

Demetrio Aguilera-Malta

Translated by

John and Carolyn Brushwood

Illustrated by

George Bartko

The Humana Press Inc. • Clifton, New Jersey

Library of Congress Cataloging in Publication Data

Main entry under title:
Aguilera Malta, Demetrio, 1909–
  Don Goyo.

  (Contemporary literature)
  Translation of Don Goyo.
  I. Title.   II. Series.
PQ8219.A36D613   863   80-81656
ISBN 0-89603-019-9

© 1980 The HUMANA Press Inc.
Crescent Manor
P. O. Box 2148
Clifton, NJ 07015

Printed in the United States of America

CONTENTS

PART ONE

CUSUMBO

I

Suddenly they heard the splashing of a canoe. Something moved in the shadow. The sound of a paddle. Then another. After that a voice—hoarse, deliberate, vigorous:

—God grant you a good evening!

—Good evening, Don Goyo.

He went slowly by, deliberately, almost by their side. The stroke of the paddle—slow, but firm—became indistinct. The enormous black boa of the night sucked him into its belly.

There was silence.

*　*　*

They had set out the *mangle,* the mangrove stakes, early, in the shifting mud of the inlet. Half men, half fish, their naked bodies—streaming, magnificent—were like the young *mangles,* veined and knotty.

The sun made a fiery rainbow on their shimmering backs. The shifting forms of their nets embraced them with an almost sexual ardor. The water offered them its spume and its waves. The canoes jumped around like unbroken colts.

They staked, tied, and went on.

The mainline of the nets rested expectantly on the bottom. The currents roared. The waves stood high. Whirlpools of fish—aimlessly thrashing around—entered the inlet. The *mangles* bent over. The cry of the *tío-tío* bird

sounded like laughter. The sun—a golden crustacean—
rested its fiery claws on the arched necks of the trees.

*   *   *

Now they were naked again. Deep in the water,
swimming—more fish than men—they raised the nets above
the level of the water. Stretched them, and made a barrier to
cut off the sudden escape of the fish.

The older of the two men spoke:

—You thrown out the mullein?

—Not yet.

—What're you waiting for? A hammerhead to break the
net? Come on! You know what the old folks say: "Shrimp
that sleep get lost in the deep."

—I'm going.

He climbed up the *ñangas,* the exposed roots, with
simian agility. Seized the flexible branches. With supreme
indifference he stepped on sharp oyster shells and taciturn
snails. Going in deeper, he followed the course of the blind
estuary. And then, there it was. He scattered the yellowish
mass of treacherous fruit—the mullein plant that poisons in
a matter of seconds. Then he bent over the water,
occasionally shaking his body when it became peppered
with a film of mosquitos.

—Damn, it's dark in here.

Even with the greatest effort he was barely able to
distinguish the whip-lines of the roots, an occasional silvery
flash of a big-headed mullet, the luminous leaping of the
dying rays, the phosphorescence of the shifting mud.

—The mullein is getting to them.

He had a feeling of anguish, a kind of fear. Momentarily
repenting, he thought it was wrong to kill them. He couldn't
even use them all. It was too much. One night's catch was

more than enough to send a canoe load to Guayaquil. The rest would stay there rotting, driving away the more precious and delicious varieties. On the other hand, the mullein respects nothing. Eventually it would kill them all—large and small. And not just the fish—the crabs, the oysters, the "mule hoofs," the "conchcrackers," the mussels, the "weepers."

* * *

A shout came up from the mouth of the estuary:
—Cusumbo!
—What?
—The tide is out. We can start.
—All right, I'm coming.
He jumped onto the *ñangas* again. Felt the crunching of the branches. Heard the croakers in the labyrinth of hanging roots. Maybe the manatee's futile call.
He reached the mouth of the estuary.
—I'm here!
They took the dipping nets from the canoe. Started pulling in the big ones. They sank in the mud to their knees. Commenced to walk slowly.
—Watch out for the wizard shrimp—or the jelly fish!
—Don't worry about me. I'm immune.
—That's what Melgar used to say before he died. Then one time a shrimp got him and laid him up for weeks...
With anxious eyes they examined the mud, especially near the bottom of the nets. There was an enormous cluster of scales in the belly of the mainline. The fish were shaking with the rhythm of death. They bunched together, friends and enemies, united before the hunger of men. They heard the noise of their ceaseless struggle with the pallid mullein. The *mangle* stakes shook vigorously. From the mud came the constant explosive noise of the dying "conchcrackers."

The last water of ebb tide dragged lazily out. The smoke made by burning ant nests was hardly enough to keep away the shower of mosquitos. It was cold. The cold that bites and scratches like a cat. The quarrelsome early morning wind was striking the mangroves on the back of the neck.

The gathering began. The dipping nets went back and forth to the canoe. The fish were already beginning to die. A few moved their red gills. But most of them fell heavily to the bottom of the canoe, lifeless. There were all kinds: porgies, yellow jacks, croakers, pompanos, mullet, corvinas, *chaparras*, bass...

Cusumbo murmured:

—Luck is running good.

—Why's that?

—No breaks in the net.

—Because we didn't catch anything big. No sharks, no alligators, no hammerheads...

—You're right.

The canoe was getting full, the canoe was riding low, the enormous canoe made of *pechiche* wood. The two *cholos*, natives of the coast, looked with sorrow on the great quantity of fish still in the estuary.

—Look at all that fish going to go bad!

—I don't think anybody's coming to get it.

—A damn shame.

They took up the nets. Dried them. Put them in another canoe half hidden in a thicket. Then, on top of everything else, they piled the *mangle* stakes.

—I wonder when those bastards are going to get here!

—It's getting late. They may not even be able to get to Guayaquil on time.

* * *

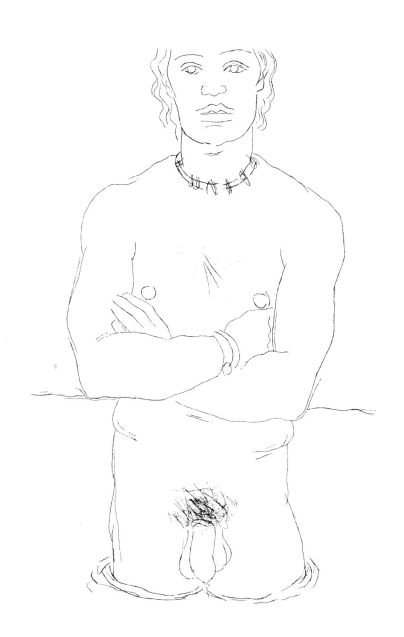

They pulled themselves into the canoe to wait. They were shivering with cold. Their bodies were still half naked. Staring into the distance, they could see beyond Big Well.

The night was growing very dark. Hardly anything was visible above the surface of the water. The punishing wind quietly invaded every corner of the islands.

—You think something has happened to them?

—I doubt it. They know these islands like the palms of their hands.

Suddenly they heard the stroke of an oar, rhythmic, strong, purposeful. It was growing louder by the moment. Now the resonant belly of the islands repeated the sound, amplifying it. They were drawing near. They were drawing near.

—There they come!

In a few minutes the canoe was alongside them. It made a crest of water that sparkled lightly in the darkness of the night.

—What happened to you?

—Nothing. We left Guayas late because it was almost dark when we ate.

—Right!

The newcomers boarded the canoe loaded with fish and the one acting as pilot commented:

—Big catch.

—And we left a good half of 'em because we couldn't get 'em in the canoe.

—That's all right.

They got into position. Then the three canoes moved away, each in its own direction. Again the firm stroke of powerful oars, and the splashing of the boats cutting the water's smooth surface with their blunt prows.

Silence fell. The islands seemed to yawn. The

mangroves initiated their millenial love-making on the soft beds of the mud.

*   *   *

There—in the cabins of the rafts—maybe they had a deerskin mat; perhaps a woman; or maybe the long awaited caress, the twisting of flesh on fire. Or it might also be the fever of lonely men.

It was miserably cold.

II

Cusumbo—as well as he could—examined himself inwardly. What was happening to him was inexplicable. He was beginning to recall scenes from his past, even some he thought he had forgotten long ago. And the strange thing was that he didn't see them as if they had happened to him, but to someone else, some other person he had known since the moment of his birth.

He was stretched out on a raft tied to the *mangles* on the bank, watching—but not really seeing—the water currents of the inlet as they duplicated the hanging *mangle* roots. He was alone. All his friends had gone to drive *mangle* stakes. He didn't want to go with them.

Almost as if he were dreaming, he remembered.

Many years ago...

*   *   *

Between the powerful thighs of a woman from the highlands—a woman he no longer even remembered—he had uttered his first cry.

It was a gray day—they told him so later. All around him were talkative old women and taciturn men. They also told him later that each one had had his say:

—He will be tough and strong like a *mangle* stake.

—Or like his mamma.

—Women will love him.

—And the men?

His mother, pleased with herself, proud of her flesh and blood, challenged them:

—He will be my son.

His father, embarrassed, forgotten in a corner of the room, didn't know what to say.

A stilettoed mosquito—with some kind of absurd eagerness to baptize him—had landed on the infant's dark red skin.

When his eyes "saw" life...

He liked stallions ridden bareback—the ones that drink the wind and the blue horizon—a horse is the canoe of the mountain. He liked resilient, proud horses that protest, that rear up; or mad horses that long to run away.

By the end of summer—the dark udders of the land laid bare as a cleared field—he rode like a cyclone, jumping over the scorched stumps, the piles of dried-up branches, the proud and robust trunks of the trees. He ran through the flames when they were burning off the land. He felt the heat of the sun on the fire-scorched pampas. The silent tamarinds and screaming carobs saw him stuck to the backs of the brutes.

From then on—he didn't know exactly when it started—he felt the impact of his name like a blow on his back:

—Cusumbo!

—Who said it first?

—Where?

—Why?

He didn't know. But he heard it over and over—behind the trees, in his home, in the town:

—Cusumbo!

—Cusumbo!

—Cusumbo!

Soon they forgot his real name. He too had forgotten it long ago.

—Cusumbo!

*   *   *

He weeded rice with a shiny snub-nosed machete, squatting between the interminable rows of tiny plants. He loved the growth of their slender leaves. He chased the iguanas, the locusts, and the *tio-tios* in the mating season. He was intoxicated by the golden heads of the grain. He liked walking in the middle of them—one more plume in the colorful fiesta of shimmering crests.

It was along the river banks washed by water at flood tide, and in the bogs seasoned with treacherous alligators, splashing like the devil, and sprinkled with waterfowl.

Immense plains—durable belts around the belly of the hills and banks—wore a brilliant, firm, and provocative yellow. Toward the end of winter, the season when the waters recede and when the inlets dry up, the victorious horses sank their vigorous hooves in the middle of the seedbed formed by the shored up banks of the rice paddies. Everything vibrated in the solar light. Everything invited him to live and to enjoy.

Ah, the spikes of grain!

And one night—most likely through a subconscious impulse—when he tried to look into himself for the first time, he gazed at the prodigious phalanx of goldengreen:

—If I could be the harvested rice!

To bring joy to the hills, and food and shelter to humankind. To feel himself both one and many—a grain of rice between the teeth, the straw the rice furnishes to cover the huts and rafts.

Ah, the golden spikes of grain!

* * *

Cusumbo milked the cows . . .

After herding them, mounted on his peppery colt, he drove the cattle, slow and silent, over the verdant pastures sprinkled here and there with dreamy carobs or *pechiches* or thick-topped tamarinds.

—Here "Jaboncillo"! Here "Mantablanca"! Hey "Diablico"! Hey, heyheyhey, hey!

The horns, high and defiant, obeyed willingly. The pasture offered itself maternally. A million green tongues licked the hanging, prodigal udders and the willing verilities. The riders waved their prods in the air threateningly. Mounted on their quick, strong horses, they made a strange line of centaurs. Spaced at intervals behind the herd, they formed a kind of human net to gather in the strays.

—Here "Jaboncillo"! Hey "Muyuyo"! Here "Fajado"! . . .

When approaching the ranch house, the first thing that they noticed was the rich smell of manure, the multiple, insistent "maaa" of the hungry calves, the hundred spots of multicolored, shimmering skin scattered about the strong corrals.

—Here "Jaboncillo"! Here "Mantablanca"! Hey "Diablico", heyheyhey! . . .

The seed bulls stayed behind the bars that closed the entrance. Their massive flesh lined up along the wire fence in a picturesque curve. The cows flooded in. They stuck their muzzles between the restraining bars as well as they could, and tenderly licked their babies, lowing gently.

Cusumbo milked the cows.

At midnight, by the light of a gasoline lantern hung high on the tallest *guayacan* tree, rainy or clear, up to his knees in mud, confused by the noisy call of the unmilked cows and by the weanlings' lament.

Cusumbo milked the cows.

He would let the eager calf take hold of the swollen teats. Would permit several attacks on the prodigal udders. And when the milk answered the call, he tied the calf by the hind legs, with a liana.

Then he squatted, pail between his legs, and his vibrating fingers squeezed the juicy clusters of flesh. The foamy stream rushed into its ample receptacle. From time to time the cow moved her foot impatiently. He knew how much milk each cow would give. And he usually left one teat unmilked for the calf.

At dawn, when the launch's whistle whipped through the hacienda, when the milk was already on its way to Guayaquil, a waterbath covering the potbellied cans, Cusumbo went up to the house and threw himself in bed.

It was possible to forget everything but Don Encarnación Estupiñán.

Don Encarnación was the focal point of all his childhood memories. Tall, sallow, bettle-browed, carrying a thick poncho over his shoulder, and armed with a dagger capable of making strong men tremble, he appeared on the hacienda occasionally and mysteriously. Everyone treated him with respect, almost with fear.

There were dozens of hair-raising tales about his adventures—jumbles of beautiful womens' skirts, brave *montuvios'*—mountainpeople's—blood, and decisive machete strokes that clipped off lives as neatly as weed stalks. Of course, nobody was absolutely certain about any of the stories that he told. And when Don Encarnación appeared, he always found a smile and a toast to his good health.

When he came down from the mountains, blustering and violent, the hacienda felt a wave of excitement. Both men and women went out to greet him:

—God grant you a good evening!

—Good evening, Don Encarnación!

Almost always he was riding a brown stallion. He dismounted in front of the first house.

—Anybody home?

—Come on in, Don Encarnación.

He tied the horse to one of the stanchions and climbed up the narrow bamboo steps. Right behind him came practically every worker on the hacienda, and their wives and children too. They all sat on the floor, observing every movement of Don Encarnación with admiration.

—Tell us a good story, Don.

—Don't know anything to tell. I've already told you all I know.

Someone suggested timidly:

—There must be one more, Don Encarna.

Don Encarnación coughed. Took off his poncho. Folded it. Rested it on his knees. He looked over his audience with satisfaction. Coughed again:

—Well, if you say so...

Speaking abruptly, in a dry, nervous style full of images, gesticulating with his hands, with his legs, with his machete, with his poncho, he began to speak.

He knew the secrets of the jungle and the secrets of the people. Like a tireless sponge absorbing the communications of people and of things, Don Encarna lived an eternal legend. He knew the language of the *guayacán* trees and of axe handles, of the fleas and of the leafy *cascole* trees, of the pumas and of the deer, of the sharks and of the giant crabs. He could also read the spirit of his comrades in their struggle against the wilderness.

And the best thing was that he was convinced that every story he told was absolutely true. If by chance someone laughed—when he was making a crocodile speak or a dead man dance in one of his tales—Don Encarna would stop talking, pick up his hat, throw his poncho over his shoulder and leave, not to return for at least a week:

—Bunch of fools...

*   *   *

One of his favorite stories—the one Cusumbo remembered best—was about Señor Francia, known as Ño Francia, and his family.

Ño Francia was a wild black loner who lived way up on the other side of Payo, miles from the hacienda house, in the middle of the mountains, completely isolated from other men. He lived with his wife and four daughters, whom he called the Little Frogs. They had been given a small piece of land to cultivate and live on, mostly to keep them from hanging around the hacienda, because people said they brought bad luck everywhere they set foot.

Ño Francia was half magician and half fortune-teller. People saw him at night, up in the tree tops or walking on the river without sinking, or spying along the side of the road, trying to cause as much trouble as he could. Nobody ever dared go to his house. And whenever a yearling or a colt wandered off in that direction, none of the workers even considered going to find it, and the animal was just given up for lost.

Well. One day the superintendent of the hacienda was

surprised to see all the laborers running in his direction, apparently frightened. He asked the first one what was happening. And he told him they had seen Ño Francia coming with his wife and four children.

—What's so bad about that?

—Ño Francia always brings bad luck.

The superintendent—a "rich man" sent to the hacienda from the city—burst out laughing.

—You dumb bastards! Still believing stuff like that!

—Its true, White Man.

In a few minutes, Ño Francia and his family were standing before the superintendent. The wild old man was nervous and upset. He looked around at all of them timidly:

—The reason I came...

—What is it?

He hesitated a while. Then looking straight at the superintendent:

—There's going to be a great wave. It's dangerous here. You and all your people, White Man, better get to the closest high ground you can find. If you don't you'll be screwed.

The superintendent laughed fit to kill.

—You're crazy.

—Have it your way, White Man. You'll see.

Immediately, before the peons could recover from the fear his warning had caused, Ño Francia and his family went straight back the way they'd come.

One of the peons spoke:

—Look, White Man. Ño Francia never lies.

—How does he know what's going to happen?

—Ño Francia knows magic. He's got an agreement with the Devil.

—Is that a fact? Well, what I'm going to do is stay right here. Anybody who wants to can go to high ground.

—All right, White Man.

The next day, the countryside was quieter than ever. The superintendent and one old person were the only ones at the hacienda house. The old man murmured:

—I know the White Man is going to screw up. But somebody ought to stay with him.

The morning had gone by without anything happening, and now it was twelve o'clock. The superintendent was sitting in his fiber hammock, looking over the railing and laughing at Ño Francia and the credulous workers. The old man sat in front of him, silent, with his head bowed, listening:

—You see? Just like I told you, nothing happened.

—Don't count your chickens yet, White Man. Ño Francia never makes a mistake.

—What a bunch of idiots...

He'd hardly said it when he noticed something strange about the mountain. And suddenly a dull, menacing roar shook his sense of security. It was the warning signal. At that instant, the jungle shook. The trees rose up, trembling. Through the midst of hanging roots, heavy thickets, and stray branches, surged an army of deer, squirrels, cows, horses, wild hogs—all the animals known in that region. They came in an absurd jumble created by terror, destroying everything in their path and even destroying themselves in their mad flight. Soon the sky grew dark. Thousands upon thousands of birds took flight, creating gigantic spots of color. The air was full of screaming, of anxious noise, of strange disturbance. And above it all, growing louder and louder, the roar of the flood waters.

The superintendent, pale, trembling, uncertain, stammered:

—He was right.

—Ño Francia never makes a mistake, White Man.

Panic took hold of them. Suddenly they were seized by

the same desire to flee that tormented the hills themselves. They nearly flew down the bamboo steps, and when they got to the bottom, the old peon murmured:

—Too late, White Man.

Gusts of a hurricane wind were striking. It seemed like the end of everything. Trees began to tremble and fall. But before hitting the ground, they commenced to walk. It was as if the jungle on the mountain had grown millions of legs. The noise was unbearable. The two men felt it through their whole bodies. Like a gigantic hand tearing at their backbones.

Suddenly, above the animals and above the trees, the great wave rose up. Spumy. Defiant. Enormous.

They did not know when the wave hit them, when it picked up the house like a plaything, when it destroyed the stanchions, when it swept it along in turn breaking it to pieces against the thousand-year-old trees. Later on, they felt themselves floating on the interminable water that stretched its monstrous arm toward the hozizon.

* * *

The following day, all the workers saw was a great lake. Everything had disappeared—the houses, the trees, the animals. From time to time the current washed up some dead cattle, already desecrated by vultures, or maybe a tree trunk or a big limb that bobbed around on the broad surface of the water. No matter how great their efforts to find the body of the White Man and the old peon, or even the hacienda house, all amounted to nothing. Who knows where the great wave took them!

—So you see—Don Encarna pointed out—what happens to unbelievers. That's why you must always believe.

The *motuvios* listened thoughtfully, without saying a

word, anxiously following every detail of his fascinating
story. When Don Encarna finished, they looked at each other
for a while, then one of them overcame his shyness and said:
—Give us another one, Don Encarna!
—That's all I've got.
—There must be something else you can tell us.
He turned his poncho around again, settling more
comfortably into his role. He looked over his audience in an
authoritative way. And continued:
—Once, in "Dos Revesas"...

* * *

It was the courageous story of an indomitable woman.
She had been born in Daule, and in Daule she started to love
and to live. They called her La Agalluda, the Greedy One,
because they say she wanting everything for herself and was
always after money. She wanted to be rich so badly it was like
an insatiable hunger gnawing at her entrails. With the help
of her undulating hips, she went about conquering all the
men, swaying like a great canoe. Nobody in town liked her.
And when she met up with one of those women who have
just one husband, always she heard her name pronounced
like an insult:
—La Agalluda.
The truth is that this woman had been deceived by a
White Man who had gone there to spend a few days. And she
had a son whom she had to provide for after being
abandoned by her seducer. And jobs were scarce in those
days. And since she had come to hate men, having lived with
only one and being always at his side . . . she did whatever she
was able to do!
Nevertheless, one day her way of life became impossible.
She had to flee downriver. And that's how she came to be in
"Dos Revesas."

"Dos Revesas" was a busy place in those days. Some gringos had come there because, according to them, there was coal and iron. They had brought a lot of machinery, and they spent every day digging into the earth with some enormous chains that were frightening to see. They employed some laborers. And La Agalluda offered to cook for them. The gringos accepted. They would give her food and lodging for herself and her child. She could live in the kitchen of the big house they had built on the river shore. She could start that very day.

La Agalluda did a lot of dreaming. She thought she could start a new life, quiet, peaceful, happy. When it was still early, she set up the mosquito net over her sleeping mat. Kissed her son and put him to bed. And she began to prepare, to the best of her ability, the food for dinner.

But that night, around twelve o'clock when everybody was sleeping, when she was resting from the day's hard work, she heard the sound of footsteps. She heard the kitchen door opening quietly. And through her net she saw the figure of a man entering the room. She couldn't contain herself:

—What are you doing here?

The man approached her forcefully and threw himself down by her side, tried to embrace her. La Agalluda, making a supreme effort, freed herself. She picked up her son, left the house, and ran toward the river.

—Damn Gringo!

She got into the first canoe she could find. Depositing her son in the bow, she pushed off. And began to row.

The night was very dark. She could distinguish absolutely nothing. She began to hear the vague shouts of the people who were telling of La Agalluda's flight. The cold penetrated to the bone. A silence reigned that was frightening. When, abruptly, they heard a long, twisting scream followed by a gentle slapping of water.

One of the eddies had pulled her under!

—Ever since then—Don Encarna concluded—all the river men who row by "Dos Revesas" cross themselves and pray for La Agalluda. Because if they don't, they see her with her baby in her arms. And she follows them all night.

When he was through, they treated Don Encarna to a shot of *puro* or a cup of coffee.

III

And one day—for Cusumbo—the inevitable happened.

It came unexpectedly, like rain on a clear day. He was eating juicy cherries under a trees. Near the bank of the river, he absentmindedly gazed out over the endless plain, burning under a heat so intense it made golden streaks in the tropical green, more peaceful than he had ever been.

Suddenly he became aware of a wild chase. Across the high canebrake he saw four sharp horns. Heard the noise of heavy breathing. The vegetation opened up before him. And "Jaboncillo" and "Fajado" came roaring out, foaming and vibrant, their flesh on fire.

They ran a long while, clumsily, stumbling over an occasional tree trunk. "Jaboncillo" fleeing, "Fajado" right behind her, potent, furious. The distances gradually shortened. Soon the bull's muzzle was near the sex of the fugitive female. One final effort. And "Fajado" jumped onto "Jaboncillo."

He heard a quiet lowing of pleasure and of pain. "Fajado" buried his insistent flesh in her. An anguished panting. "Jaboncillo" trembled. A slender thread of the milk of creation fell to the ground, absurdly wasted. It was all very fast, like a thunderclap of tormented flesh. They vibrated, moaning, electrified, in the midst of the wondering pasture, the leaning trees, the astonished water.

So—turned into a single tidal wave of muscle—they disappeared into the green of the *janeiro* grass and continued along the most difficult trails in a titanic act of fecundity.

Cusumbo, astonished, ecstatic, began to understand.

*   *   *

It was a kind of awakening. Bathing and watching the other hacienda children bathe, he began to form an analogy between himself and "Fajado," and between "Jaboncillo" and many of the little girls he played with. His flesh cried out. His surroundings became a burning celebration. He stretched and peered over the panorama of his life to examine the inviting horizon. And, in spite of all, he felt alone—like a snail in the ravine of life—his blood shaken by a ferocious desire for initiation.

He no longer had a moment of peace. Often he got lost in the hills, looking for something he never found. He went out in his canoe, heading downstream, stretched out on the bottom, hoping, always hoping. Often at night—when everybody else was snoring—he would get up. He would go to the cane door—the one toward the canals—trembling, not knowing what was happening to him, but noticing that the cold air had a calming effect.

However, when he saw the cattle close together in countless groups, he sensed the warmth of so much flesh, and felt even lonelier among the multitude of females. He could hardly contain himself.

—If I could be a seed bull!

Not to worry about anything, not to have to do anything. Just penetrate the dark flesh of the females and the green flesh of the *janeiro* grass. Squander his sap—useless today—like the seed of the multitudes. Protect all the herd against the claws and sharp teeth of the jaguar. To live a life of power and of domination over all the pasture.

—If I could be a seed bull!

* * *

What he waited for so long finally happened.

One time his parents went to visit some old friends and took him along. The friends' house was up river, on the other side of Babahoyo. They needed a really favorable tide to get there.

There was a party at the friends' house. They danced on the cane floor. A drunk was singing a love song. The guitar seemed to cry when his alcoholic hand strummed its cords. Couples, blended in close and violent embrace, smelled of liquor, of desire, of dizziness. Liquor, the seasoning of *montuvio* revelry, reared in their eyes and lashed their flesh.

It seemed that the house, imitating the rhythm of the people, began to dance. All its ancient wood warbled. And its *bijao* leaves moved back and forth gently to the tune of the country music.

Suddenly someone yelled:

—And Cusumbo doesn't dance?

He answered shyly:

—No. Not me.

The old man, half drunk already and staggering, took him by the hand and led him across the room:

—Come on, bashful, learn.

It was like an explosion.

—Yeah, go on and dance.

—Sure, go on and learn.

—Dance, man, dance!

He tried to make excuses:

—I never danced before.

—No? Then Nica can show you how. Come here, Nica, and teach this boy to dance.

Nica came over. She was the daughter of the people who owned the house. A little older than Cusumbo, her swelling maturity was apparent under the rough *saraza* cloth she was wearing. She took the youth by the hand.

—Let's dance, Cusumbo!

—I don't know how!

—Come, man, learn! You afraid of me?

The whole crowd of *montuvios* gathered round. Began to urge them on:

—Right. Go on and dance!

—Nica, show him how.

—Don't be bashful!

—Go on and dance!

—Dance, Cusumbo. The girl isn't going to hurt you. That did it.

—All right.

* * *

It was getting dark.

In the corner, the lamp commenced to open its luminous eyes. Strokes of shadow brushed themselves on all things. The lines of the bamboo faded into darkness. Couples drifted off from the rest of the crowd.

Cusumbo danced, holding on to Nica, pressed against her, not knowing where his feet were or what they were doing. Half drunk, even though he hadn't touched a drop of *puro*, he felt the gentle pressure of her whole female body. The house was revolving around him. A strange sensation gradually came over him and now he truly was afraid.

As they made a turn near the steps, Nica spoke very slowly:

—Listen, Cusumbo, I have to go downstairs. Want to come with me? It's dark there and I'm afraid to go by myself. Want to come?

—All right.

Slowly they went down the steps. None of the *montuvios*—drunk by this time—noticed they were leaving.

Still the overwrought guitar poured forth its clamor of confused and disparate notes. Voices raucous with liquor joined the singer in the chorus. The house trembled. Outside, night sank its black teeth into the fertile belly of the earth.

*   *   *

A dialog rose out of the darkness:

—Where are you going?

—This way.

—You want me to go there with you?

—No, this way is better.

—All right, then.

She looked at him closely, trying to guess what he was thinking. Then she laughed and kept on walking down the narrow path toward the Manantial spring. She walked slowly, deliberately, her accessible behind swaying temptingly.

Cusumbo followed her step by step, holding his breath, looking, listening, trying to guess her movements. In a little while he heard the sound of clothes being rumpled. He went closer. He was able to see her squatting.

In a flash of memory he saw "Jaboncillo" and "Fajado," their vibrant mass, the sorrowful and joyous lowing, the possession, the convulsive gallop of the grinding pair.

And...

He could no longer control himself!

He jumped like a jaguar. Seized her. Pressed himself to her body. Whispered, almost in spite of himself:

—Nica...

She tried to get free, to straighten her still-loosened clothing. She struggled fiercely for a while.

And yet...

—Nica...I want...

—Get away from me! Leave me alone!

—I can't...

He pressed her to him. Closer, closer. She began to respond. She was trembling now. She made no effort to defend herself.

—Cusumbo.

Now she held him close. Unexpectedly kissed him. The boy grew crimson.

—Cusumbo.

—Nica.

—Not here. Come. Under the tamarind is better.

Cusumbo couldn't see a thing.

* * *

And under the tamarind, he spoke to her as if she were a cow.

—Back up, Nica.

—Here I am.

—No, not that way.

She was lying there, face up, offering herself to him. Her clothing, pulled up over her belly, left her body plainly visible. Cusumbo investigated her avidly with his hands.

—How, then?

—This way, as the cows get ready for the bull.

—No, that's not right. Understand? That's not the way.

—Yes it is. The other day I watched "Fajado" and "Jaboncillo."

—But... wait... animals are different. Haven't you ever done it?

—No. Never.

—Oh. Well that's different.

She guided him. Helped him. He felt a sharp and violent pain. But...

—You see, Cusumbo?

—Yes.

The wind shook the leaves of the trees. The moon stuck out its placid face. From the *montuvios'* house came the half-drunk strumming of the guitar and the discordant voice of the drunken singer.

IV

He was becoming a man.

Little by little his body was fleshing out and his muscles hardening. He felt as strong as a bull. The hills had instilled in him a strange rebelliousness, an unsatisfied appetite for endless competition, the overbearing attitude of an unbroken colt. With his machete in hand, he feared neither God nor the devil. Living in the constant agitation of sap spilling over. Pricking holes in the horizon, always challenging.

But one day the Old Man beat Cusumbo's mother to death. He had come home drunk, swearing under his breath, staggering, had climbed the steps, for the first time in his life domineering. Had planted himself in the middle of the house. Had crossed his arms.

—Nobody's going to fuck me!

He roared. Spit. His bloodshot eyes searched everywhere. His unending timidity had finally been overcome. He snorted like an animal.

—I said nobody is going to fuck me! I'm sick and tired of taking it from everybody! I'm going to screw somebody myself. Only way to get along around here is to screw somebody else. The boss draws my blood from me; now I'm going to treat all of you to a few kicks!

His eyes were getting redder and redder, like burning coals. He took a few steps forward. And really began to beat them brutally. The Old Woman—she had been sick for several days—couldn't defend herself. He—Cusumbo—received a few blows himself.

* * *

For the first time, he looked carefully at the world around him. He looked at the endless planted fields; the rice paddies loaded with grain; the voluptuous *janeiro* grass alive with colorful spots of cattle; the land stretching into distance as great as the sky; the crouching peons humbly nourishing their land with sweat and blood, land prodigal in fruit never theirs; the boss, potbellied and proud, always on horseback, always with an insult on his lips and a whip in his hand.

Cusumbo understood. He had never had a childhood, or games, or happiness. He remembered that his hands had never been free of the weeding hoe, or the oar, or the horse's reins at roundup. He couldn't remember at what age he had started to work. Maybe the day he was born. And always under the constant threat of beatings from the Old Man or the boss.

He envied the trees, free out on the endless plains; and the birds, flying wherever they wished; and the horses, stretched out in a wild gallop, bolting for the horizon; the water, always moving onward.

Now his jobs were heavier, much harder. They lasted longer. He was assigned more cows to milk. By daybreak he had to be squatting with a pot-bellied jar between his legs, bitten by mosquitos that landed on him in clouds. While it was still early morning he had to lead the cows out to pasture. His legs were bowed from so much riding. In the afternoon, if there was no hoeing, he had to round up stray cattle. Or he commenced riding over the endless pastures.

*   *   *

The Old Man was drinking more than ever. And he was hardly able to work at all. After the death of his wife, he hung around the saloons every day. And drank, and drank, and drank without rest until he toppled over in a stupor. When he came to, he would go to work. And he bent to the job, working like a mule, for a while, until he made enough money to get drunk again. He no longer cared about anything. Staring myopically at everything around him, he acted as if he were sleepwalking.

One day he called Cusumbo and, to the latter's astonishment, said:

—You know, Cusumbo? We're screwed. Screwed for the rest of our lives.

—Why, Old Man?

He hesitated a moment. Dropped his gaze. Lowered his eyes. Spoke haltingly:

—When I married your mamma, I asked the Boss to lend me some money. It was around two hundred *sucres*. You know. Everybody around here does that. We had a few things to buy then. And that loan increased the debt I inherited from my own Old Man. You understand?

—Yes, Old Man.

—Good. Since then I haven't been able to pay off hardly any of it. At least that's what the White Man says. Food costs a lot. His pay is low. And a little drink now and then...

—I understand, Old Man.

He stopped talking, as if he didn't know quite what to say. Cusumbo helped him.

—What else, Old Man?

—Well...the Boss called me in today...And he told me: "Look at it this way, Old Man: you are never going to be able to pay me. You're old. You drink too much. You will die very soon. Your son is going to have to take over your debt. If he doesn't, I'm going to have you put in jail." And I said, "All right, Boss."

Cusumbo recognized the inevitable.

—I'll pay it, Old Man. Don't worry about it.

And that was exactly what happened. He started paying. The Old Man died. And he kept on paying. A new White Man came to the hacienda. And he kept on paying. Then winter. Then another. And he kept on paying. Stump pullers and mechanized seeders came to the hacienda. Many of the workers were dismissed. But Cusumbo kept on paying. Every day, every week, every month, every year.

It was like a rosary of labors. The Boss's demanding voice was always after him:

—Cusumbo. Get to the weeding. The rice is almost grown over.

—All right, Boss.

From morning to night, squatting, clearing the rows between the gracefully tapered plants, under the sun or in the rain, sweating, panting, grumbling in silence of his sorrow and his bad luck, distractedly aware of the flight of the *tio-tios,* until the bell rang announcing the end of the day's work.

And when he got back to the house, the whip-like voice of the Master:

—Cusumbo. Go get the cattle. By yourself. You don't need any help.

Riding a frisky horse, practically bareback, his knees aching. Having to chase after the wandering cows. Ducking thorny branches every moment. Seeing night come, the hills grow silent, and quietness flood across the land. And having to run, half anesthetized by his overwhelming fatigue.

And then, back at the house again:

—Cusumbo, go catch some fish, a few *bocachicos*. But hurry back. It's almost dark.

—All right, Boss.

Rowing, seated in the stern. Rowing when his arms and legs were aching, when his ass was raw, when hunger and fatigue were sinking their teeth into all his muscles. Rowing, until he reached the place where he would climb up to fish. Rowing, feeling the paddle grow many times heavier. And then waiting, waiting a long time for a fish to come close so he could trap it. Waiting, while night turned everything black, while the penetrating cold licked at his bones. Waiting until he could return with the string of coveted fish.

And when he got back, still that same damned voice:

—Cusumbo. Cut me a little carob wood. We don't have enough to heat the coffee tomorrow morning.

—All right, Boss.

Slinging the axe over his shoulder. Going to look for fallen trees, as close as possible. Maybe having to go a long way to find them. And then beginning to chop, feeling his arms coming out of the joints, that the axe was growing to weigh a ton. And returning to the house, loaded down— splinters torturing his back—with the bundles of chopped wood.

—All right, Boss.

Half asleep while falling into bed. And when it seems he's going to rest. When his eyes close and everything becomes dim, then fades away, that voice again:

—Time to milk the cows.

* * *

Sometimes, there in the heart of the forest, when he went deer hunting, there among the gigantic trees, the strange noises, and the wild animals, he started thinking. He did not understand what was happening to him. He was no longer as sure of himself as he had been in other times. He felt inexplicably afraid of everything. It seemed he encountered a precipice no matter which way he turned. It was as if his flesh were shrinking, deflating ironically, only to show the angular ridges of his bones, poorly covered by the protuberances of better times. He no longer stroked his machete lovingly, and he could have sworn it was no longer the faithful companion it used to be.

Sometimes he would feel unexpectedly rebellious. He would go to the White Man. Stand up to him. Violently scream: "Nobody is going to fuck me. I'm tired of putting up with you. I'd rather get a bullet in the heart than let you screw me like this." Then he would pounce, he would pounce on him like a jaguar. Let him have some steel in his belly. And afterwards, of course . . . They'd probably cut him to pieces. But the truth was that he had changed a lot. He had suffered so much and worked so much that he had become a pitiful weakling. A wretch not good for anything but kissing the White Man's ass.

At other times he had an urge to run away. To jump over the jungles and rivers. To strike out for parts unknown. To be able to work at whatever he wished. To live his own life at last, his poor, unendingly mistreated, downtrodden life. He was even afraid to run away. It was the panic of his eternal exploitation, the vengeance of the earth over which his ancestors had been lords and masters. And so he stayed, passive, silent, humble, forebearing, lower than any animal on the hacienda.

* * *

Instinctively he knew they were cheating him. Every Saturday he went to the hacienda house to get his pay. Standing in front of a table covered with papers that had writing he couldn't understand, behind whose fortifications stood the White Man, Cusumbo listened to the eternal chant:

—You owe me three hundred, you earned fifty, you pay me thirty. That leaves you owing me two hundred and ninety.

—All right, Boss.

Humbly he went downstairs, with his head bowed, not looking at anybody, ashamed of himself.

* * *

One fine day he heard the ancestral call of the saloon. The bottles danced before his eyes, temptingly lined up on their shelves. He began to drink to forget and soon was drinking to be drinking. It was a sort of outrageous possession. His thirst for liquor pulled him like a daily and inevitable magnet. His eyes grew bloodshot. His pulse irregular. He abandoned himself completely, and the stoop of his shoulders revealed his condition. He hated the forest, his fellow workers, the cows, everything around him. He could think of nothing but the clear, burning liquid that transported him, and changed everything for him.

The Boss called him in several times. He spoke to him in a voice that was sharp and serious:

—Cusumbo, you're drinking too much. You're not paying off a thing. Your debt's growing. You're never going to be able to pay it.

—All right, Boss.

—I can't lend you any more money, or help you anymore, in any way.

—All right, Boss.

V

There was one bright spot in the darkness of his life. He had Nica.

Ever since she awakened him to the celebration of sex, her dark passion had excited him. From afar, he watched her gradual development. Often at night he couldn't sleep for thinking about her body, imagining how much he would enjoy having her there beside him. Even in those moments when he was drunkest, he saw her walking around him, sensuous, undulating.

He had rarely been close to her since that first time. She seemed to avoid him, although she might cast a smile or a provocative glance in his direction. They never said more than a few words to each other:

—You're a nice piece.

—They say you drink too much.

—I like you better than ever.

—You're going to ruin youself.

—I'm going to get you for myself.

But one evening it really happened. He rowed his canoe up to her Old Man's farm. He called out. Nica came down from the house and looked over the bank:

—What do you want?

—Come on down. I've got something to tell you.

—What is it?

—Come on down here so I can tell you.

—Okay, I'm coming. But be careful...

Soon she was beside the canoe, standing on the balsa poles that served as a dock. Once again he admired the dark, vibrant skin he could guess under the coarse dress stuck to her body.

—What's going on?

He commenced to explore her avidly with his eyes. It was difficult for him to speak:

—Well...I want you to come live with me...

Nica threw back her head and burst out laughing.

—Don't be...

He lowered his head and continued speaking:

—With me you won't lack for a thing. I can do any kind of work. Men say I'm strong and women that I'm brave too. And I really like you a lot.

Nica went on bellowing with laughter. He couldn't bear it. He jumped out of the canoe. Leapt over to her. Pressed her against his body. It all happened so rapidly that she had no time to escape him.

—You're coming with me.

She tried to protest. Wriggled nervously.

—Wait! I'll go, but wait.

—For what?

—Let me go get my clothes.

—Forget it. You're going with me right now. I'll come get whatever you want later.

Nica raised her head. Stared at him attentively for a long time. And murmured:

—All right.

*   *   *

He decided to be good, on her account; to work hard, on her account. Making a great effort, he was able to stay away from the saloons. He devoted himself wholeheartedly to his work. Once more life filled his robust breast, made him eager to win the daily struggle, painted a smile on the lips that had been bitter and warped by sorrow. He made peace with the forest. Every Sunday he went hunting, always bringing home first-class game.

His work was probably even harder than before; the struggle more difficult. Perhaps the White Man was crueler than before. Maybe his debt had grown unbelieveably. But now all his troubles were eclipsed by Nica's body. No matter where he was, he was always thinking about the moment when they would be together again—those short nights of pure delight.

They had given him a tiny house, with a single room, on the bank of the river, half hidden in a thicket. And Nica waited for him there every night.

As soon as they finished dinner, Nica sat on the *petate* mat. And Cusumbo stretched out laying his head in her lap. And they talked for a long time, making plans for the future, when he would have finished paying the White Man, when they would have children, when the children would be grown up, and when he and she would be old...

The hours passed without their noticing it, until it was time to milk. And then, in the corral, beside the impatient cow, he thought only about Nica and the moment he would be free to see her again.

When he went back—after finishing all his work for the day—those were the best times. Then, when Nica turned into pure passion, he forgot everything else and felt powerful and fertile, like an animal from the mountains.

*　*　*

Several months passed. He figured he had at last found happiness. He forgot the debt hanging over him. Searched for a way to get along with the White Man. Pardoned his constant cruelty. Decided that not everybody is equal in this life: that some are destined to exploit and trample on others. And the White Man was one of the exploiters. He volunteered to farm a small piece of land, with his wife's help, where they raised all kinds of vegetables. His happiness had so mellowed his spirit he accepted everything with a smile.

But one day...

When he was going, with his machete in hand, to do some weeding, he heard laughter behind him. He turned. And saw a group of his fellow workers staring at him mockingly. His head swam. His blood throbbed. Instinctively he brandished the shaft of his machete. In an instant, he had restrained himself. Why would they be laughing at him? Maybe it didn't even have anything to do with him. He continued tranquilly down the road. Without saying a word to them.

On the next day, when they were all at work, he heard the same insulting laughter again. And this time there was no doubt they were laughing at him. He raised his head. Shook his machete. Rushed over to them.

—What the hell is going on?

They stopped talking, stared at him, astonished. One of them stammered:

—Nothing... we were telling some jokes.

After the first moment, they recovered. The ironic smiles again appeared on their faces. They recovered their taunting attitude.

—Good, and now, what are you worried about?

He held himself in check. Thought of Nica. Lowered his head.

—If you weren't laughing at me, I'm not worried about anything.

That afternoon he was peacefully returning home when somebody caught up with him and grabbed him violently by the shoulder, shaking him. He turned.

—Well, Cusumbo, what's wrong with you?

—Me? Nothing. What do you mean?

The man hesitated a moment. Until finally, he could not hold it back. And the sentences struck Cusumbo like machete blows:

—I don't like to be the one to tell you. But I don't like to see a man get screwed either. You don't know what's happening? The White Man is laying your woman!

Cusumbo jumped. Knocked him down. Started to choke him. He was livid, convulsed, blind with rage:

—Bastard!

The other man struggled in vain to free himself. Began to hear his own labored breathing.

—Bastard!

Making a final effort, the man gave details:

—Every day, while you're rounding up cattle, the White Man goes to see her.

Everything turned cloudy and dark. Mechanically, Cusumbo started walking.

* * *

The dirty little whore!

But could it really be true? How could what he had heard be true? He couldn't believe it. His excited thoughts reviewed all of their caresses. The feverishly mad nights when she vibrated like a guitar beneath his volcanic body. Her peaceful expression, always lovely. The rightness of her open thighs awaiting the thrust of his virile spike, his planter of seed.

He couldn't believe it!

Suddenly he understood the laughter of all those days. The ironic glances that had pursued him. The insulting remarks that had pounded his ears. And he felt a searing flame in every cell.

He went back into the forest. Began to walk around in a daze. Envied again the gigantic and powerful trees. Eternal masters of the earth-female, sinewy and strong, secure in their place, they shake out their leafy hair over the shoulders of the horizon. He envied the iguanas zigzagging over the pigweed and the tiny purslane, the sharp-beaked *punta-de-estaca* bird that jeers at the eternal tragedy of the forest, perched atop a pole and looking like part of the wood itself; even the shaggy, clumsy porcupine making its prickly way over the torrid land.

He thought. No. He couldn't condemn Nica this way. He had to see with his own eyes, so that he wouldn't have the slightest doubt. He would go home. Act as if he suspected nothing. Spend that night—maybe the last night—in her arms. For the last time, he would plant his fertilizing seed in her. He would tremble with the pleasure of this dance, lying above her thighs, her belly, her breasts.

Next day...

At four o'clock in the afternoon, after making sure his machete would come out of its sheath easily, when he figured they would think he was most completely lost in his work, riding over the burning pastures, he suddenly set out at a gallop.

It was a kind of farewell. It seemed that the trees spoke to him gravely from alongside the path. He watched them go by in an endless procession, dancing screams of rage, their polyform coiffures trembling with emotion. A caress of hope rose up from the earth. Possibly its thousand wrinkled mouths guessed the odor of blood. The dust turned into clouds trying to catch him.

He got there before he realized where he was. In two leaps he climbed the stairs. And once there, was blinded by rage.

* * *

All this—even after so many years—he remembered perfectly. What happened after that was blurred in a series of superimposed images, macabre, absurd, disjointed. Sometimes it was like a whirlwind in his hand. A whirlwind of steel that cut and cut into dark flesh and into white flesh. Then a sea of blood covering faces, covering whole bodies. Cries of anguish, of sorrow, of supplication; insults, curses, moans. Two bodies that stop quivering. A long hesitation. The forebears who jump over their blood. A whole race protesting. The mad flight, crossing the mountain, crossing the rivers. Stung by mosquitos. Watched by the snakes, by the jaguars, by the wild hogs. Hunger. Hunger. Maddening hunger. Delirium. Fury. Thirst. Fever. Hunger. Does the sun exist? Is there a God? Am I still alive? Which way to go? Hunger. The mountain, an octopus. Vampire mountain. Mountain and hunger. Am I still alive?

* * *

At last, the islands. Without knowing how, freedom. And fishing. Fishing in the silvery, peaceful estuaries: the Rural Police could not find him there.

VI

It was already late. They hadn't caught many fish. So . . .

They turned the prow back toward Cerrito de los Morreños. Day was breaking. The estuary, in the sway of the tide, carried them along as if they were flying. Once in a while they had to move the paddle, mainly to keep going in the right direction. A soft breeze made the light green water slightly choppy. The endless line of the mangroves, the *mangles*, seemed to be dressing themselves with clouds. From time to time a gannet, flying slowly and silently, passed very close to the canoe. From the shore constantly came the resonant and monotonous "crack" of the *conchaprieta* shells opening up among the mass of roots. It was cold.

Tomás Leitón broke the silence:

—Cusumbo?

—What?

—Do you think they'll have any bananas?

—Maybe. The sloop "Mercedes Orgelina" just came into port yesterday.

—Damn. If they don't we're screwed. Me, without bananas!

—And, me!

They were rounding the curve at Los Colorados. Now they could see the little hummock of land called Cerrito de los Morreños. With its bald top—circled by the catlike *mangles* along the shore—they said it looked like a gigantic monk's head. The estuary opened out a little and became choppier. Slowly everything was becoming visible.

Don Leitón spoke again:

—Cusumbo!

—What?

The old man tried to approach him as closely as possible. In a mysterious tone, half trembling, he murmured:

—I think Don Goyo has been speaking with the Devil.

—Don't be stupid, Don Leitón.

The old man stopped rowing. Looked straight at Cusumbo. Then his sailor's eye wandered out over the distant islands, which were barely a gray line above the surface of the estuary.

—You remember the night Doña Paula died? It was dark as I've ever seen it. I could see nothing. I was scared. I swear to God, I was scared. I was rowing just as hard as I could. I headed for El Empalado. All of a sudden I heard a canoe coming up behind me. I turned. Saw it coming, coming, bringing a crest of water under its prow. I stopped. And the canoe passed me like a gust of wind. My teeth chattered. I saw no one. But I heard Don Goyo's voice: "Good evening." And then later, the stroke of the paddle, slow, strong. The wave almost swamped me. Swear to God, I nearly screamed. And generally I'm not afraid of any man!

—That's the way to be!

—And the other night, when we were out hunting ... All of us saw him right at El Empalado. We were moving slowly. The moon was bright. We could see as well as in daylight. What we were doing was telling stories about the highlands and ... When suddenly we saw Don Goyo perched up in a mangrove like a monkey, without a stitch of clothes on, his flesh looking as if it had been washed and wrung out, so tough he didn't mind mosquitos or the sharp oysters or anything. He looked like he had his prick stuck to the *mangle* ... He looked at us. Laughed a laugh that would chill your bones. We ran away from there like crazy men ...

The sun began to climb over the backbone of the islands like a golden crab. Its presence could be sensed in the yellow fiesta of thick-topped mangroves, in the increasing clarity of the atmosphere, in the diminishing cold.

* * *

They reached Cerrito. A crowd of women and children came down from the only two houses there, carrying trays under their arms:

—God grant you a good day!

—Good day.

As they stopped, the canoe turned halfway around. They surrounded it. All of them started talking at the same time:

—How much is this corvina, Cusumbo?

—How much is this dogfish, Cusumbo?

—How much is this bass?

—These mullet?

—This croaker?

—These *chaparras?*

Everybody was reaching into the belly of the canoe, where the fish were covered with water. Grabbing the piece most to their liking. Lifting it high before Cusumbo's eyes, and asking the standard questions. Even now, in the bottom of the canoe, on top of the tangle of scales, they saw an occasional live fish, red gills trembling and trying to escape one last time.

Cusumbo stated the prices. Usually he had to change them because they all wanted to haggle and get the fish for half what he had asked. Among the customers was a girl who had caught his attention, and who had looked attentively back at him, holding up a bass.

—Cusumbo, how much is this bass?

—Three *reales.*

—But it's just a small one.

—No, it's a good one. Look again.

The girl held it out, testing its weight.

—Absurd. It's too much.

—All right. You can have it for two and a half.

—No. That's still too much. Anyway, you ought to give it to me.

Cusumbo laughed.

—And you? What are you giving me?

—You? Nothing. What could I give you?

Cusumbo looked straight at her. And laughed again.

—All right, then. Take it. But tell me your name.

—Gertrudis Quimi. They call me Gertru.

—Right.

The fish were moving from the canoe to the trays that the women were carrying in their arms. They had bought them cheap and had enough food for several days.

—They're fresh.

The smell of fish was beating incessantly all along the shore. It was a strong, penetrating odor. Some say the *cholos'* bodies smell of it, and their souls too.

* * *

Once the selling was finished, they went ashore. The dogs came out to meet them. Started to bark and jump all around the two men. Someone yelled from the nearest house:

—Call off the dogs!

—Down "Leal"!

—Down "Vencedor"!

—Down!

The dogs continued barking as if they had heard nothing. Cusumbo and Don Leitón walked on.

—Good day, Doña Andrea.

—Good day.

—How are you today?

—Fair, thank you. And you?

—Getting along, no more.

—Come in. Why not come in?

—Then we will.

Quickly they climbed up the bamboo ladder. It was the first time Cusumbo had been in this house. He looked around carefully.

The house was large; all the material was split bamboo, nailed on a mangrove-beam frame. There were no partitions, no walls. Everything in it was piled up as if it had been forgotten. There were several braziers made from kerosene drums lined with clay; many half-pitched mosquito nets; bunches of green cooking bananas hanging everywhere; sacks of rice in the corners; hammocks, axes, nets, all in disarray. In the center of the house were some *cholo* peasants beside their squatting women or leaning against them while being deloused.

—Good day!

—Same to you.

Doña Andrea—still opulant in spite of her advanced years—came forward:

—Well, how've you been getting along?

Don Leitón answered:

—Well...last night we had a tear in the nets. And because of that lost almost all the fish. So we got screwed. When we got it fixed, it was already too late. And anyway, we didn't have much of a catch.

—Right.

—Now we want to buy some bananas.

—Fine. How many?

—Two bunches.

—O.K. Come take a look.

They didn't waste much time deciding. Picked up the first ones they saw.

—These.

—Good. They're worth two *sucres*.

—All right.

Cusumbo paid and was about to pitch the two bunches over his shoulders when he heard a voice:

—How about a cup of coffee?

Gertru was standing behind them laughing.

—Fine.

—It'll be ready in a minute. I'll fry you some bananas. I'll mash them and make them into dumplings.

—Much obliged, Gertru.

And Cusumbo, who was devouring her with his eyes:

—I tell you, Doña Andrea, that girl is really something. I think I'll make you my mother-in-law.

The old woman laughed.

—Tell her about it. As for me... That's what women are born to do... Too bad for anybody who doesn't try it...

—That's right, Doña Andrea.

They were drinking coffee, seated on two crates. Delicious. It stained the enameled metal cups. The banana dumpling, juicy and yellow, opened like a flower—cooking bananas are islanders' bread—

Cusumbo commented:

—Listen, Gertru. This is good...

—What is?

—The coffee... and your stuff too.

—You know, you're...

The sun—indiscreetly—commenced to peek through the windows of the house. Everything was illuminated. El Cerrito stuck its bald pate up over the fiesta of *mangles*. It was turning hot as the devil, heat that bit into the timbers, making them creak. The inlet seemed to be quietly boiling.

Cusumbo continued:

—Listen Gertru...

—What?

—Will you marry me?

The *chola* looked at him carefully for a moment. Then laughed.

—No!

—And why not?

—Because the man I marry has to be a mangrove cutter. Didn't you know that?

—No, I didn't...

—My father is a mangrove cutter, a *manglero*. My grandfather is a *manglero*. My brothers are *mangleros*. Everybody here—from the time they are born—is a *manglero*. They learn to swing an axe while still in their mother's womb.

—That's true.

—And I have to marry a *manglero*.

—All right, then.

He took the last sip of coffee. Looked somewhat thoughtful. Gertru reinforced her point:

—Anyway. You don't even play the guitar . . . or sing. So . . .

—You're right.

They stood up. Each man threw a bunch of bananas over his shoulders. And started down the steps.

—Goodbye, Doña Andrea. Goodbye and thanks a lot, Gertru.

—Goodbye.

—Goodbye. You're welcome.

*   *   *

—The man I marry has to be . . .

Although he didn't know why, that simple statement hurt him. It was as if a thorn had sunk its point deep in his flesh. Maybe even worse. As if a wild mare had kicked him mercilessly.

—The man I marry has to be . . .

He was rowing furiously. The sun whipping his vibrant muscles with fire. The canoe forced its way—like a large shark—through the motionless water. The *mangles* bent toward them. The voiceless murmur of hot blood pullulated all along the shore.

Don Leitón looked at Cusumbo ironically. Finally, he couldn't hold his tongue:

—Cusumbo!

—What?

—You've fallen in love with Gertru, haven't you?

—Yes.

—Well, you're in trouble. These women here are very screwed up. If you want one of them, you have to become a *manglero*. If not, she won't give you a whiff...

—Right.

—The man I marry has to be...

*   *   *

On the other hand.... There are lots of women! In Guayaquil at least...

And one morning, in his fishing canoe, eager and feeling strong as a bull, he set out for Guayaquil, via the dozens of estuaries...

When they saw him leaving, his *cholo* working companions murmured with hidden envy:

—Cusumbo is horny as hell.

VII

They reached Guayaquil via the Estero Salado. Put in at Puerto Duarte, not far from American Park, which they could see in the distance, full of bathers.

Guayaquil was awakening into the full swing of daily life. A distant hivelike buzzing reached their ears. Smoke

from dozens of small coal ovens arose from the outskirts of
the city, plumed the shore. As the growing light swept away
dawn, the streets yawned and stretched, and the houses
opened the eyelids of their windows.

They tied the canoe to the first dock. Emptied out the
fish for the street hawkers who were waiting. Then they half
washed the canoe. And after that, with difficulty, by
exercising superhuman effort, they put on their shoes, put
on clean shirts, dabbed a few drops of water on their faces,
and went ashore.

One of them grumbled:

—Let's go in. And take the streetcar.

—No. Let's walk. It's better.

—Don't act so dumb. Let's get the streetcar. It's a long
way!

—The other shore. We have some business over there.

—All right, then. Let's go.

They went through the middle of the slums on the
outskirts of the city, all wooden houses. Traveled over the
dirty and neglected streets, breathing the noxious putrid air
around them.

—They ought to call this place Puerto Stink.

—For sure.

They reached the curve made by the Sucre-Vélez
streetcar. Waited a few minutes. Soon they heard the
growling of the motor, and a little later the vehicle they
wanted came into view.

—It looks like a palm worm.

It came to a halt, half trembling, and they got on and
paid their fare. The streetcar started moving again.

Cusumbo felt uncomfortable. He twisted around
nervously in his seat. Looked all around him. Sweated. Felt
hostile toward everything he saw.

—Damn the luck that makes me go anywhere on four wheels! ...

The streetcar picked up speed. The houses went by more rapidly. Melted into each other. As they penetrated deeper into the city, the houses seemed to grow increasingly finer, and after a time were exceedingly large. An unusual feeling of dejection grew in Cusumbo's spirit. He felt diminished, humiliated by so much height and beauty, so much speed and strength. As if to convince himself, he murmured:

—My mare was better than this.

The streetcar started slowing down. Sharp noises flavored the atmosphere. Now the life of the street was more apparent, constantly increasing. Innumerable men peppered the street corners. Others crowded the doorways, loaded down with cans of milk or sacks of bread. Now and then a truck delivering ice or food. The outlines of things became clearer. Colón Street showed off its clean-lined, elegant buildings of wood or reinforced concrete, lavish in solid colors and handsome. Now Cusumbo felt half seduced by the city.

—Some day I'm going to live in Guayaquil!

* * *

They got off at the corner of Sucre and Pedro Carbo. Hesitating, they stood in the middle of the street, not knowing where to go. A passing automobile almost brushed them.

—Bastard!

Cusumbo asked impatiently:

—Well? Which way do we go?

—To the shore of the Guayas. We'll go to El Conchero. And from there to La Tahona.

—Right.

They walked slowly, bumping into everybody. Went as far as Pichincha, and from there toward Villamil.

They breathed deeply. Cusumbo—without knowing why—murmured:

—This is more like it!

The big old houses seemed to be dancing a dance of neglect. Their sleepy old timbers were leaning, breaking, falling. Patches of old paint adhered like treacherous hands to the ancestral prodigies of the walls. It was easy to imagine some elegant colonial Don Juan emerging from one of the rickety doorways; or a lady looking out from the House of a Hundred Windows, nervously witnessing a duel at the corner; or perhaps even a sorrowful love song offered at the foot of the House of the Columns. The fragrance of yesterday became emotion, even in the least significant of stones bordering the doorways, as if fleeing the noise of civilization.

—Ah, Villamil! . . .

That's where you find the small shopkeepers; saloons and misery; the sleepy nodding of a dying epoch; the half briny smell of a seaport atmosphere; the moaning guitars stuck in corners; the rags of flesh that drag themselves along the murmuring sidewalks.

—Ah, Villamil! . . .

* * *

La Tahona:

Mountain of sacked coal. The din of men, sloops, and wharves. The Guayas River rampant with strong currents. The saloons half open and waiting. Women smiling and offering themselves. A strange odor of sweaty and panting flesh. Occasionally the squeaking of a cart. Perhaps the uproar of a few men fighting. The whole seaport fiesta became a song of flesh and motion.

The fishermen went into the shop of an Italian.

—Good morning.

—Good morning. What can I do for you?

—We want to do a little shopping.

—Sure. Whatever you like.

The man waiting on them was a clerk. But the Italian, as soon as he saw them enter, took the clerk aside. And told him:

—These *cholos* are very stupid. You can overcharge them and get away with it.

—O.K.

The *cholos* asked for some rice, lard, salt, bananas, sugar, frijoles, lentils, and a few other items.

The clerk put it all down on a piece of paper. In fact, he put down anything he wanted to. When he finished, he told them:

—Here it is. It comes to fifteen *sucres.*

The *cholos* paid without questioning. Rented a burro. And loaded the supplies on him for the trip to Puerto Duarte. One of them accompanied the quadruped. The others kept on wandering along the shore, finally ending up in a saloon. They stationed themselves at the bar and started drinking.

* * *

The liquor—cane turned into fire—gradually got into their blood. Things acquired strange and ridiculous qualities in their simple minds. They felt—as if on a stormy night—they were aboard a wallowing sloop. The bottles appeared in waves. Waves that got deep within them, filling them with the rhythm of the sea.

Liquor.

... Coal, coal filling the streets, coal on their shoulders, filling their lives; coal, black coal, white coal, flesh coal, woman coal; smoke that brings fire; fire running in their veins; someone raises up the bar, the men; fire only women can quench; the canoe, what time does the canoe leave...

Cusumbo grew enraged:

—Nobody fucks me!

And another voice:

—Me either!

Cusumbo—under the influence of alcohol—wanted to fight.

—Son of a bitch. I'll let you taste a little steel. Goddamn you!

The fishermen held him back. And after struggling a few moments, they persuaded him not to get into a brawl.

—Don't be a fool. Come on. What you need is a woman.

—No, damnit. I'm going to screw whatever I see.

—Let's go back. Come on. Let's go!

They took him out by force. And outside...

Wharves opening their pants; the sloops are whores; the sloops surrendering to all the wharves; clouds going to bed because they're hot; coal filling the streets; men are stupid bastards because the streets have so much land; Guayaquil ought to be in the islands because everything is getting so dark; damn the sun for making you sweat out all the liquor...

—Cusumbo is drunk.

—We're all half shot...

The city was sparkling with life. Noise and movement everywhere. Everyone hurrying to earn his daily bread. Even the streets appeared to be moving. The streetcars hummed in the distance. Automobiles rushed over the wide macadam. There was a strange, pleasant smell of rain.

—We're all half drunk!

They were making *z*'s and *x*'s as they staggered along. Hardly able to stand. Holding onto each other for security.

* * *

They took the Sucre-Vélez streetcar again. Half asleep, they watched the endless line of houses move past. They reached San Francisco Plaza where the streetcar stopped for a moment. And then continued its noisy journey down Vélez Street. Intimidated by their surroundings, the fishermen hardly spoke at all. A strange languor was beginning to lap their vertebrae when one of them muttered:

—We're there.

They got off. They were on a highly questionable street. Hesitating, they continued slowly on their staggering hike, hardly able to distinguish what was around them. They got mixed up in the confusion of the surrounding streets. Started to search, and then one of them—somewhat more knowledgeable than the rest—said:

—Here it is...

They had stopped in front of a tiny little house, dirty and creaking, with human rags against all the walls—a strange gray little house that inspired pity. They knocked and soon the melancholy voice of a woman called:

—Come in!

VIII

When Cusumbo came fully to himself, they were on their way back to the islands. From time to time he heard the vigorous strokes of the powerful oarsmen. Probably six hours had gone by, maybe more. It was night. Growing very dark. The *ñangas*—the hanging roots of the *mangles* in the estuary they were crossing—looked like the claws of antediluvian monsters. It was cold. He was leaning over the rail used to hang the nets. The canoe was sliding along, smoothly cutting the surface of the water. The rowing of the men seemed to grow stronger and stronger.

Cusumbo tried to remember what had happened. His head was aching. Something was throbbing, but he didn't know where. He would have sworn he had a fever. Somebody at his side said hoarsely:

—You really cut loose...

Then his subconscious brought it all back clearly. And standing apart from himself—as if it had all happened to somebody else—he saw:

Saw how he threw himself on top of a naked woman with sagging, pitiful flesh; how he churned on top of her, fiercely impelled by the liquor; how his own flesh felt repelled, and offended, bathed him in a gelatinous lethargy.

Feeling nauseated, he muttered:

—I don't like those Guayas women.

In the distance, the manatee seemed to rise up among the hanging *mangle* roots. The "crack" of the bivalves was sounding loudly. From time to time, a silvery school of bigheaded mullet crossed in front of them, like a cluster of arrows. A gentle breeze began to roughen the surface of the inlet's water. The moon above—a flickering moon just come up, like a piece of theatre scenery—seemed to climb over the back of the islands.

Suddenly they could hear the beat of a paddle, slow but firm, the movement of the water and the hanging mangrove roots, a strange, mysterious breeze.

—God grant you a good evening!

—Good evening, Don Goyo.

Deliberately, slowly, he went by, almost by their side.

Their powerful hands gripped the oars anxiously. Their eyes stared unwavering into the darkness. The mangroves on the island echoed back:

—Good evening, Don Goyo.

Several days later—when he was in the estuary, completely nude and half submerged, driving stakes in order to put out the nets—he felt a sharp pain in his privates. It was as if the long spike of a jaguar's claw had pierced him, cutting deeply, very deeply into his most tender flesh.

He didn't think it was important. Kept on working. Waited patiently for the ebb tide, stretched out in the canoe, burning under the sun's caress. But when he went to urinate over the side of the canoe, he couldn't stand it. A hornet wouldn't have stung any worse. And the liquid that came out was yellow, thick, and stinking.

—Goddamn it!

He remembered when he was still a kid in the highlands country, they had told him:

—Never go near those Guayas whores. A lot of them have clap.

Goddamn it. Had he really caught the stuff? He felt like running, screaming, climbing into one of the canoes going to Guayaquil. And then find the woman who had screwed him. Kick her in the ass. Beat her up so she wouldn't give it to anybody else. But he calmed down. Maybe nothing was wrong with him. Perhaps it was the liquor. Maybe some insect had stung him. Or maybe some poisonous grass. Or too much work. Who knows what!

He didn't tell anybody about it. Kept on working as usual. Put out the nets and waited for the flood tide. Hauled in the nets. Threw out the mullein. Caught many fish. Everything went along fine. The canoes went to Guayaquil.

He stayed there alone in the whirlwind of the islands.

* * *

On the following day he got up early while it was still half dark. And the first thing he did was look at himself.

No longer any doubt about it. He was in trouble, he definitely had it. He was disgusted with himself. All his clothes were stained. His member burned like a fire coal. The liquid had turned green, thick, bloody.

When he went to urinate, he choked back a scream. He urinated slowly making a supreme effort, almost a drop at a time, holding on to the hanging *mangle* roots, cursing and complaining.

He worked all day, as usual. Repeated the daily leaps into the stooping *mangles*. Once more he worked on the fabric of the nets. Sank deep into the silent water. Helped bring in the fish and to pull up the stakes. As if nothing had happened to him.

But he deteriorated. The pain became unbearable. He couldn't stand it. Before all the *cholo* fishermen he told his secret:

—The Guayas whore stung me.

—If you want, we can cure you here. If not, go see a doctor in Guayaquil.

If he went to Guayaquil he could see the woman who gave it to him. And in spite of all, he didn't quite trust the *cholo* remedies.

So it was that he went to Guayaquil again.

* * *

They took him to a big house where a lot of people were hurrying in and out. It was like an ant hill. From time to time he bumped into women dressed in blue who wore white wings like heron's on their heads. Many men wearing glasses were acting very important. And innumerable skinny, pale, sad types were coming and going, quietly and thoughtfully.

—This is the hospital.

—All right.

—Let's go in.

—I'm afraid of it.

He hesitated a while; but finally made the decision. That's what he had come for. He wasn't going to act like a beggar now that he'd started to do it. And after all, he wouldn't be the first or the last.

He went in.

They made him wait several hours, sitting in a room with a few other people. Every so often a door opened, and the people who were waiting went in gradually. Cusumbo was leaking urine. And he also felt a strange anxiety gnawing his whole body. He was sweating profusely. The people around him moved away, disturbed by his stink and his clothing all stained with filth and *mangle*.

When it was already late, almost dark, the door opened one last time. A woman appeared.

—The rest of you will have to come back tomorrow. Office hours are over for today.

—All right.

Everybody began to leave the room. As they moved, they swept Cusumbo and his friend along with them:

—O.K. But what's going on?

—I don't know. They say office hours are over.

—What a lousy trick. And me pissing all over myself.

—Hold it. We're getting out right now.

But he didn't have time.

And...

The insult came from the other end of the corridor:

—*Cholo* swine!

The others watched them leave and ridicule poured from every set of eyes and lips. Cusumbo was ashen, taciturn, unaware of what he was seeing or where he was walking.

—Goddamn them!

*   *   *

How many days did Cusumbo go back? How many days did they treat him? He lost count. He was half somnambulant. Little by little he had grown accustomed to his illness. He hardly noticed it. The doctors had also become familiar with Cusumbo, always quiet and serious.

One day they told him he would have to be hospitalized. His testicles were swollen. Things were going from bad to worse. Above all, they said, because he couldn't take proper care of himself. But he didn't get any better in the hospital either. And soon he was bored.

Day after day, the persistent bathing with silver nitrate. The dull, stupid food, as if made for the White Men or for their women. Sometimes they stuck him. Vaguely, as if he were dreaming, he saw them taking away the dead from the beds nearby. Everything blurred, ran together. He had to tap himself on the head to be convinced he was awake.

*   *   *

One fine day they told him that he was better and that somebody else needed his bed. That he could take care of himself. A little surprised, he left uncertainly. Went out not knowing where to go. His companions had not returned to see him. He started up the first street he came to.

Better? Were they making fun of him? He knew perfectly well he was in practically the same condition as when he went there, maybe even worse. The White Man's doctors hadn't helped him a bit.

Unexpectedly he bumped into somebody.

—Cusumbo!

He looked up. Stared. He thought he was dreaming, but this time it was real.

—Gertru!

Gertru and Ña Andrea were examining him from head to foot.

—Damn, you're skinny.

—I just got out of the hospital.

—I see. Are you better?

—Much worse than I was before.

—I'm not surprised. Don Goyo would have cured you long ago. If you want me to, I'll take you where he is. He'll treat you right there.

—All right, then.

* * *

Don Goyo treated him. He made him drink plantain water that had been left to season through several night dews. He injected boiled lime juice through his urethra, making him jump. He fixed who knows how many other brews. And cured him.

Cusumbo developed a hatred for women, even though the blood throbbed in his veins. He hated liquor too, because it blinded him. And he hated the city and the whites. He bought a huge axe, second hand, and a guitar.

—I'm going to cut *mangle*.

But—once again, goddamn it, once again—he thought of the *chola*. That Gertru, she's a woman isn't she?

—The man I marry has to be . . .

PART TWO

THE MANGROVES DISAPPEAR

I

Doña Andrea poured out another glass of liquor:

—Drink up, Don Carlos... for the little dead girl. The poor tiny girl is probably in heaven by now!.... So delicate she was!...

—Thank you, Ña Andrea.

With a certain amount of repugnance, he lifted the glass. But after the first shock was over, the liquor flowed down smoothly.

The *cholos* were dancing wildly on the bamboo floor—the party at its height—dressed in an indescribable color, barefoot, each one holding a bottle, or a woman, or maybe just a straw hat.

In the corner a guitar was screaming, accompanying the hard, strange voice of a half-drunk singer. In the opposite corner, mounted on two ironing boards, was a box in which rested the "poor tiny dead girl."

She had died that afternoon. Died of what? Of nothing. Or almost nothing... She was bewitched... Some unknown sinner with the "evil eye" had looked at her. And it's clear. That's what had to be... They had taken the poor little thing somewhere... She—Ña Andrea—thought probably to heaven. But if that's not the way things work out?... And if the devil himself carried her off?... In the end... you have to hope for the best... God helps those who believe in him.

—Pour yourself another drink, Don Carlos.

The White Man protested:

—I believe I've had enough, Ña Andrea.

—I doubt it, White Man. But if you don't want to drink with us poor people...

77

He made an effort. Stuck out his hand.

—Well, then, if you insist. But it's the last one.

* * *

Over there—a few steps from the house—the waters of Three Mouth Inlet were raging. Roaring. They spit their wavy insults over the muddy shore. They desperately tried to wash out the stakes to which the canoes and sloops were moored. They mounted the high mangrove trunks, the *mangles*, transformed into climbing vines of spume. And then—persuaded of the futility of their efforts—hurtled back upon themselves.

It was cold. The liquor commenced to give the wake a strange animation. Four lamps, one in each corner, illuminated the single-room house. There were thirty men and twenty women.

And who knows how many bottles.

* * *

—You know something?

—What?

—Next week I'm going to kidnap you so we can get married.

—All right...

He held her passionately against his body. He made her feel a strange tickling between her thighs. She protested:

—Don't be so rough! You're messing up my dress!

Gertru's shoes resounded on the bamboo floor in an outburst of joy—all the joy of her eager body. She felt Cusumbo pushing against her, pressing his body to hers harder and harder. But she couldn't stop him. She liked it. She liked it too much. And anyway, weren't they going to be

married soon? Hadn't they promised each other a long time ago?

Cusumbo brought his cheek as near to hers as he could. And he whispered near her ear!

—Listen, Gertru... Don Carlos is talking with Don Goyo a lot. That's not good. Don Carlos is a very evil man. You don't know him. But up river he has a bad reputation. They say he's quieted more than one!

—You mean he's killed some people?

—That's what they say.

What did she care about Don Carlos and Don Goyo? Even though Don Goyo was her father, the only thing that mattered to her—now—was her Cusumbo. The only thing she wanted was to sleep—and not only sleep—with him under the same net, on the same deerskin. Let Don Carlos and Don Goyo talk as much as they wanted to...

She felt full of herself. Sensing more than ever the strength of love guided only by instinct. She felt it in her breasts, firm and mobile. Throughout her whole body, which she had never given to anyone.

The guitar kept on sounding its confused, incoherent notes. The dancing grew more enthusiastic, more animated. The couples pressed closer together as they whirled. A strange odor of brazen flesh began to flicker in the atmosphere.

When no one expected it, someone bellowed:

—Here's to the future bride and groom!

* * *

Don Carlos—the White Man—must have been about thirty years old. Nobody knew where he came from. They figured he was a *gringo* because he didn't talk like the other whites in Guayaquil. They said he was evil, completely evil,

like all the whites. That he had come to the islands to cheat
the *cholos*. He was tall and strong. Wore leggings. Looked
tough. Wore khaki clothing.

Don Goyo Quimi—the progenitor of the island
people—was probably a hundred and forty or fifty years old,
so they said. His children and grandchildren looked like his
brothers. His skin, wrinkled and hard, was like the skin of
dried fruit. Half bent over he walked slowly and with
difficulty. But in the water—what a difference. He seemed
like a fish. He managed the canoe as might any of his great
grandchildren. He could handle the harpoon or the trident.
Handled the casting net. Tended the stationary net. He
played tricks on the tiger sharks. "They are my friends," he
always said.

Ña Andrea—Don Goyo's latest wife—kept the glass in
her hand:

—Help yourself, Old Man... Help yourself, Don
Carlos. It's good *puro*. Made from the best cane you can get
from up above Daule... It's never hurt anybody.

The White Man—already half drunk—stopped short.

—All right then, damn it... But give me the bottle!

Ña Andrea laughed:

—And they say white men don't like to drink.

It was green, green as hope. And it was full, completely
full. Strong as a southwester. But white men have tough
throats. And Don Carlos drank the whole bottle without
stopping.

He smacked his lips. Stared myopically at all the *cholos*.
Stood before Ña Andrea and laughed:

—It's all right. Damn it!

The *cholo* partying kept right on. The "poor tiny dead
girl" wore an ironic expression. The lamps were growing
dim. Men were beginning to drop. The guitar sounded
sleepy. The wake inspired sorrow and fear, an unusual wake
for a little girl who had been "evil-eyed."

The inlet glistened like a sharp machete. From time to time, he listened to the lazy noise of the sloops and canoes, dancing on the moving bed of restless water. Then, in the distance, San Ignacio, the island that had fresh water, seemed to want to speak. The undertow muttered among the *ñanga* roots like a parrot.

II

They had gone outside quietly, without anybody noticing. Now they were sitting on a *mangle* trunk, on the edge of the bank, sensing the water almost lapping their feet. Indifferently they watched the canoes breaking the waves, illuminated by the profile of a first-quarter moon. They pressed closely together, as if engraved on each other.
Cusumbo spoke:
—Do you remember, Gertru?
—Remember what?
—What I said to you that time . . .
—Oh, that . . . No! No, I don't remember!
—Yes, you do. But you don't want to say so.
—No. I swear to god. I don't remember!
It was cold there, a cold that pierced their bones, that seemed to thrust a million small needles under both their young skins. The inlet began to quiet down.
The *mangles* seemed to bend over, smiling, to listen to them. The north wind blew earnestly, awkwardly, blowing their clothing close against their bodies, and then shaking it out, as if it were trying to undress them.
—Well *I* remember. As if it were this very day.
—Well . . .
She remembered too. Of course . . . How could she forget

so soon! She was just pretending to have forgotten. She
enjoyed seeing Cusumbo this way.

—It was in San Miguel del Morro. Don't you remember?

—No. I don't remember.

—No? Don't you remember your father had gone to get
some peons for the White Man?

—Yes, I remember that.

—Don't you remember that you went with him?

—Yes. But what's that got to do with...?

Cusumbo was growing excited. His words were
pushing each other through his lips:

—Well, nothing. I've liked you since I first saw you. You
remember? Here in Cerrito de los Morreños. When I came to
sell fish and you served me some coffee and a banana
dumpling. When you told me that if I wanted you I'd have to
be a *manglero*. And strum the guitar a little... Well ever
since then...

—What?

—Now I'm a *manglero*. And I learned to sing and to
play... Remember?

—No. Nothing!

—When you went to San Miguel, I went there too.

—Oh, you did?

—I started hanging around the sloop "Mercedes
Orgelina." Keeping an eye on you night and day. Playing
the guitar a little. To see if it said anything to you.

—That's not true.

—No, it's pure truth. As God is my witness.

They nestled closer. Almost unconsciously they started
kissing. His clumsy hands fumbled under her clothing. The
chola protested:

—No. Don't do that.

Cusumbo, blind with passion, tried to force her. He
pushed up against her with his body strong as a *mangle*

trunk. He pressed her tightly in his arms. Made her feel his wild virility.

—No, you animal . . . Let me go or I'll scream!

—Just for a moment . . .

—No . . . I mean no.

—Don't be cruel, Gertru!

—Cruel because I don't let you fool with me?

—But we know we're going to get married.

—Exactly.

—All right, then.

He felt an insane impulse to strike her, to throw her to the earth, to stamp on her, to spit in her face, to rip off her clothes, to humiliate her. And then—having conquered her and put her in her place—to say:

—You know, you little bitch? . . . I don't love you.

But it was only a lightning flash. In a minute, his tone changed. Weakening, he murmured gently:

—You are right, Gertru. It's better to wait.

She—with the gentleness of a sheltered inlet—took his arm. And almost whispered:

—You got heated up, Cusumbo? . . . That was wrong . . . Because all I was thinking of was your good . . . You know what they say: "If you let them try the fruit, they may not buy the fruit." . . . And what if you should forget me then, Cusumbo . . . It would disgrace you and disgrace me . . . Then nobody could love you as much as I love you . . . Nobody could wait for you to come home from cutting *mangle* the way I could wait for you . . . I'll have your supper ready. The deerskin fresh . . . And I'll always be ready to please you . . . You got heated up, Cusumbo?

—Not really, Gertru . . . it's just that when I'm with you I get prickles all over me, and a dizziness that I can't explain. . . . But I'm all right now . . . See?

They nestled against each other again, almost without

being aware of it. They pressed close—one to the other—not caring that the inlet below them was laughing at their plans, not caring about the sharp, cruel cold, nor caring about the wake up at the house, striking a strange note in the gray melody of the islands.

* * *

And the wake continued. Of course. They had to celebrate well for "the poor, tiny dead girl." If they didn't, she might even go off to Hell. The evil way christians act these days.

The *puro* was vibrating—like a guitar—in the souls of the *cholos*. Their drunkenness gave them the look of faded images in an etching. They fell against each other, in complete oblivion. Muttered crazy phrases extracted from their pitiful brains, as if from a synthesis of personalities...

—You know, you old bastard?...Sunday I'm leaving for Guayas...I'm weary of everything...Goddamn it all...Everybody owes me...I get so mad...I need fifty *sucres*. Damn it all!

—Where the hell is that flat-nosed Nicomedes? I'm going to take his woman out.

—Stick to what's yours, you bastard!

—Nobody's going to screw me. I'm telling you.

When he tried to move, the man fell.

—Goddamn it!

Suddenly a voice came up from the floor:

—Ask Cusumbo to sing!

—Ask Cusumbo!

—Ask Cusumbo!

—Ask Cusumbo!

They rapidly looked around and didn't see him. Then they began to call:

—Cusumbo!

—Cusumbo, come and sing!

—Cusumbo!

Somebody noticed that Gertru was also missing. And then everybody laughed.

—By damn! I think Cusumbo is out laying Gertru. I don't see either of them.

Don Goyo—from one of the corners—objected:

—Don't speak ill of the boy! He's worth more than the rest of you together.

He had not finished speaking when Gertru and Cusumbo appeared.

—Here they are. I know my people!

Cusumbo asked:

—Well, what's going on?

—Nothing. We just want you to sing something.

—But it's already very late.

—No, no. Go on and sing!

—Go on and sing!

They handed him the guitar. He had to agree. And he began to strum. For a moment there was complete silence. The people gathered themselves together. And Cusumbo sang.

It was a old song poorly learned, a mixture of strong island rhythm with a weary city tone. It seemed to communicate the sorrowful life of a people who were disappearing. The music adhered to the *cholos'* backs like a whiplash. They listened to it sadly.

—That's a very sad song.

—Sad songs are the best.

—I like the ones about drinking and fighting more.

—They're even worse.

∗   ∗   ∗

The wake continued. Now it was nearly dawn. As if foreshadowing the proximity of light, the night became even darker. The inlet glittered like a tree of silver printed on the black undergrowth of the islands.

Don Carlos—who could no longer stand up—babbled:

—Somebody take me home.

—All right, White Man. I'll take you.

And Don Goyo Quimî—the oldest *cholo* on the islands—pushed him forward.

The wake continued...The humble wake of the tiny girl who had been "evil-eyed."

III

The canoe moved slowly. Of course. Don Goyo was piloting...And Don Goyo moved the paddle very little. He permitted the current to carry him, with the strange bearing of a sphinx kneaded from the dark mud of numberless ravines.

He seemed to be sleeping. His thorax swelled. His sinewy hands gripped the rugged oar with an air of dominance. The canoe—although slowly—kept moving forward while Don Carlos snored peacefully in the prow.

The darkness grew more and more intense. There wasn't a star in the sky. The thick-laced *mangles* seemed to weave their branches into the shadows. Gigantic silhouettes rose up from the inlet like a herd of enormous prehistoric triceratops. There wasn't a "drop" of wind. Silence was absolute.

Don Goyo—the patriarch of five generations—was afraid; deeply and absurdly afraid, as he had never been before, with a fear that settled in his throat, that gave him an insane longing to scream, to run and lose himself in the labyrinth of branches and hanging roots.

And Don Goyo—who had never been afraid—when he felt afraid for the first time, wept.

Two tears, like two knife wounds, opened tragic furrows in the jungle of wrinkles on his face.

Abruptly—at one of the turns of the estuary, near El Empalado—they heard a tremendous crunching. Everything shook. A lash of anguish hung over the water. A strange breath of sorrow permeated the atmosphere. The islands' backbone twisted, heaving up. Astonished, ecstatic, the palms raised up. The millions of *ñangas* roots engraved themselves on the feverish mud. And then, calm. Absolute, impassive calm that penetrated all things.

The oldest *mangle* on the islands—one that Don Goyo had watched grow up with him—bent over. Its greenish-black leaves seemed to caress the ancient *cholo*. Its bark opened up like a gigantic flower. Its seamed knots looked like entrails torn out. And before the astonished centuries, grown restless with sorrow and life—the oldest mangle on the islands—its voice strange and sad spoke:

—We are going away, Don Goyo. Going away. The evil White Man has come. Has come to uproot us from the earth we were born in, has come to corrupt us with gold that makes slaves, has come to make us enemies of each other, even though your race and mine have always lived together, and always were loving and beloved. Today our mutilated bodies bleed constantly. They skin away our bark, our only shelter. Sometimes—most times—they don't even use us. They leave us lying in the mud, abandoned.

The word echoed in the remotest corners of the islands:

—Abandoned!

—Abandoned!

—Abandoned!

The *mangles* seemed to come together, near the one who

spoke. The current halted. Don Goyo would have liked to cry
out. He couldn't breathe. He was sweating profusely.
Trembling. His poor flesh rocking like a hammock.

The oldest *mangle* on the islands continued speaking:

—Ah, Goyo! If only I could run; leave this unfriendly
place; loose my heavy roots and my innumerable hanging
arms. If only I could sink myself in the soil of other islands
still not profaned, in order not to witness the death of what I
have loved most. If only I could climb over the past like a
monstrous spider or bury myself in the ocean where I was
born and spent my childhood... Ah, Goyo old friend,
eternal compañero, if I could only run!... if I could only
flee!

The *cholo* felt feverish. He looked around, his eyes
disoriented, not knowing what to do. The canoe had
stopped. It seemed that the inlet opened up and a thousand
kinds of fish emerged from its bosom, that they stared
mockingly at Don Goyo, at Don Goyo, *cholo* patriarch of
five generations.

The oldest *mangle* on the islands spoke again:

—But that really is not what I want. The truth is I would
not be able to leave, Goyo. I could not leave you alone, my
brother whom I have known from birth and always
protected. I cannot, Goyo, cannot.... And, then, you are a
manglero. You live by our death. I have sworn to be faithful
to you and to yours. I don't care whether I fall under your
axe, or the axe of your people, in order to provide you shelter
or food, or to help you in any of your needs... But the White
Men! Ah, Goyo!... The White Men will strip the islands
bare... They will uproot your people too. Your men, like
rags of flesh, will one day cast themselves into the ocean.

The old *mangle's* voice grew louder, louder. Like a
cyclone, it seemed to pound the colossal torso of the islands.

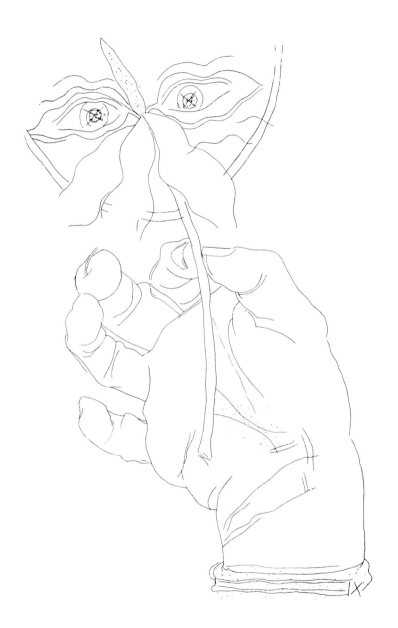

A peculiar unrestrained anguish leavened the expectant moment. Don Goyo felt thirsty.

The moon came out briefly to listen. The blood of the *mangles* coursed through the hammock of the waves. A shark, or perhaps a hammerhead, slashed the trembling surface of the water like a steel dagger.

Don Carlos woke up.

*   *   *

Don Goyo wondered if he had been dreaming. But within, he didn't know where, but deep within, he sensed something counseling him, even ordering him, to believe what he had seen and heard. And in fact, what his old friend the *mangle* had said was, after all, what he had been thinking for a long time. Slowly he came to understand that was what the White Men wanted when they had come to work on the islands: to rob the *cholos* of what was theirs; to make them work for the White Man's benefit; to wait quietly in their houses for the *cholos* to bring them stumpwood or firewood or *mangle* bark, so they could buy it for a pittance and then sell it for much more in Guayaquil. Yes, it was true, undoubtedly true. The day would come when there wouldn't be a stick of *mangle* left, nor a place on the islands in which the poor *cholos* could live. They would have to take refuge in the sea, and live on rafts or sloops, or emigrate to the hateful cities where you can't breathe.

But no, he would stop it in time. He would not allow his sons or his grandsons or any of his people to work for the White Men any longer, or to cut a single *mangle*. And he could do it! Beginning that day he would declare war to the death against those gluttonous whites who wanted everything for themselves.

The islands would once again be planted with rustling palms. The tides would bring the floating seeds, no longer fearfully, and plant them in the soft beds of mud. Each island would be filled with gentlefolk. Men and *mangles* would be friends again, closer than ever. They would live and work together, each helping the other.

The gluttonous whites would see...

*   *   *

For the first time he rowed vigorously. Jabbed the paddle with a machete-like stroke. His muscles swelled. His veins trembled with anger as the blood rushed through them. The canoe broke the water. It drank the horizon in quick gulps. The speed of his anguish written in spume.

Don Carlos asked:

—What time is it?

Don Goyo would have gladly thrown him into the water. It was all so tranquil, so peaceful. No one would ever know. He would say that the canoe had reared before a strong wind, that Don Carlos had fallen out, and since he was too drunk, had not been able to swim. All of Don Goyo's attempts to rescue him had proved fruitless... He felt repentant. No. He would not fight that way. He would always fight openly, honestly, calmly. Anyway, nothing would be achieved by the death of this White Man since there were so many more...

—I don't know.

The air was growing heavy, unusually heavy. It was difficult for him to breathe. It seemed as if the air were filled with the blood of the mangroves.

In the distance, they heard dogs barking. They had arrived.

IV

The axe rang like a bell as it fell on the trunks. Slowly the *mangles* weakened under its incessant caress. They opened up in bloody chips. Trembled. Roared. Seemed to stretch, trying to take in one last breath of wind, and then, finally—with a convulsive tremor—they fell into the brutal arms of distance, dragging down millions of elastic *ñangas* and intricately woven branches.

The scream of their tortured cells flew like a hurricane rider. The islands' discontent traveled through the atmosphere. The sun's warmth set fire to the heart of the mangrove cutter. Countless flashes of bright orange were fixed against a fiesta of eager leaves. The manatees talked along the shore line. The *cholos,* between strokes of the axe, sweating profusely, half naked, spoke:

—You know, I'm getting married next month and I could use a little money. And now, working for the White Man, I can earn a little. So...

—You're right. It's good to have a woman. And Gertru is one of the best...

—No doubt about it. Next month I'm going to take her to Guayas. I've got a little money already. So...

—I don't blame you...

The flood tide was a claw tearing at the robust udders of the hanging roots. The current, the force of the water, had the driftwood dancing. A strong north wind began to blow. The axe seemed to fall harder. The *mangles* were falling— one after another—in an endless rosary of broken joints. The *cholos* seemed to be monolithic sphinxes. From time to time a flash of light on their bodies responded to the sun's dull signal.

* * *

Now the axe—biting stubbornly into the dead *mangle* wood—was dipping into the water. The tide flooded the *ñangas* quickly. They heard the constant "crack" of the closing mollusks. Snails and spider crabs made their way up to the highest branches. The mosquitos came in waves that cast shadows. The smoke of burning ant hills was not enough to restrain them. The canoes were far out on the water, moored to their *mangle* stakes.

Don Leitón murmured:

—We have to go back.

The *mangles* were cut into logs of almost exactly the same length, rough, twisted, bleeding. First they had trimmed off the branches; then cleaned the piece they most desired. All this while performing acrobatic prodigies over the immense ramifications of crooked and slippery wood.

They started loading the canoes. Each man took a piece, lifted it on his shoulders, and carried it to the boat. They made several trips. And then in a few moments the canoes were loaded. The *cholos* boarded them and began to row.

There was no wind. The water was still. The inlet, in the sun's embrace, turned a milky copper color. It seemed silently to boil. The *mangles* began sweating onto the banks. The current of full tide was slacking. In the distance, the hills of Chongón struck their outline clearly against the pure blue sky. The canoes dragged along lazily. The *cholos* felt the tropical lassitude like a woman's caress on the napes of their necks.

*   *   *

Old man Leitón spoke:

—The *mangle* tree is a part of us. We have it inside.

And he tried to explain.

The *mangles* had slowly been working out a dominant

position, one of possessing men, circuitously, silently, conceivably without the *cholos* noticing. *Mangles* had strange powers unknown to men: pliable and invisible branches that grow through the flesh, through the eyes, through the mouths, through the hair of all men, branches that root themselves in life, that attach themselves—like climbing vines—to the sleeping skin of the island. Ah, the *mangles*...

And then he said:

—Every time I swung the axe today to fell a *mangle*, I felt as if I were cutting myself down.

And it was natural. Who knows how many of the branches he had destroyed had been bonds between himself and the trees? Perhaps some of the palm seed he destroyed was his own, or maybe a handful of the finest dark green leaves.

The *cholos* looked at him and laughed, not understanding. Finally, Cusumbo asked:

—And you, how do you know all that?

—I found it out living with the *mangle*, learning to observe all the little things carefully. And I've seen more...

—What?

—When the *mangles* are screwing the islands.

—Stop lying, Don Leitón!

—I'm not lying. It's the truth! I've watched them many nights, everybody was asleep. First it appears that the *mangles* start to dance. From a distance you can watch them shaking their branches. They make a terrifying noise. Everything gets quiet in order to see and hear more. The islands start trembling enough to make the water dance.

The more Don Leitón talked, the more enthusiastic he became. Gradually the *cholos* had stopped laughing. Now they were listening attentively to the tale of the talkative old man. Don Leitón continued:

—Then all of a sudden the *mangles* stuck themselves right into the islands, like a million boar hogs.

It was a strange fiesta of nuptial convulsions. The sinewy bridegrooms were stretching themselves. They were panting thunderously in an outpouring of virility. They looked like vertical swordfish, enormous *catanudos*, *catanudos* turned into an earthquake of lust and a fury of rushing water. Then, the orgasm, the seed, the humble, wild seed that would float, abandoned, over the ocean, until it encountered another mate-mother island where it could take on life and give its sap in return.

The little hill thrust its bald, shiny head above the gray-green forest of the scorching islands.

* * *

When they arrived, Don Goyo was waiting for them on the shore. And Don Goyo, with his trembling and sad voice, spoke to them:

—We must cut no more *mangle*!

All of them made gestures of protest. Puzzled, they looked at each other, trying to understand. Then, questioning silently, they turned toward the enigmatic old man.

Don Goyo tried to explain:

—The *mangles* are like a part of us.

Yes, even though all of them might doubt it, the poor *mangles* could see, hear, speak, and feel. Every blow of the axe made the *mangle* grow pale with pain, just like a man. They complained. Protested. Even tried to run away. But they were manacled to the islands. And, of course, their language was not understandable to men.

—The *mangles* are just like us...

He—Don Goyo—had learned it clearly the night before. The oldest *mangle* on the island had told him so. They had spoken a long time, when he was taking the White Man home. His friend the tree had complained that the *cholos*, men of his own kind, his brothers, were cutting them down so outsiders could profit, often leaving them abandoned and scorned in the treacherous mud, alongside the fallen timber. Almost in tears, he had begged Don Goyo that no more *mangle* be cut, that they dedicate themselves to fishing, or crabbing, or anything.

* * *

The full tide had greatly swollen the inlet. White-capped waves crawled onto the shore. Women came out of their houses to listen. Dogs looked half sad. Canoes murmured quietly.

Don Goyo was finishing his speech:

— ... So you see. We have to catch fish or crabs. Never again cut *mangle*! It is as if we were cutting ourselves down. What's more, we must hate the White Man! Struggle against the cursed and gluttonous White Man who wants everything for himself. The Whites are like the flood tide. Little by little a million hungry tongues lick away at the *ñangas*, at the islands, until they have disappeared. Someday we ourselves will disappear ... We will fish with the harpoon or the spear, with casting nets or with staking nets, in the shallows or in the deep.

V

That night Gertru and Cusumbo went down from the house very early. With tremulous steps they headed toward the shore. They found one of the thickest *mangle* trunks and sat down. The tide was rising. They were just above the water. The moon began to stick out its pale face. Silvery scars snaked over the mobile skin of the inlet. A strange confusion of noises came from the nearby *mangle* groves. A strong north wind was blowing gently.

Glued to each other, they began to talk:

—That's right, Gertru. Don Goyo wants it. We're going to fish.

—Sounds like bad news to me. Everything will go wrong. You watch!

—I think you're right. For me, anyway...

—And for me...You remember? When we first met I told you: "Everybody in my family is a *manglero*. You have to be a *manglero*. If not...

—Sure. And now look. We have to change it all around. I did it all for nothing...stopped fishing...went to Don Leitón...had to work hard to convince him. Now we have to go back the other way.

The tide was climbing up the *ñanga* thickets. The wind cut their cheeks. There, in the distance, three dolphins were jumping.

Cusumbo turned optimistic:

—No matter, Gertru. You'll see. I've been a fisherman before. You can make money. You'll see. As soon as we get a little money saved up, we'll get married. You'll see.

—Maybe. But I'd rather have you cutting *mangle*.

—You're right. But Don Goyo says that he knows the *mangles* are like us, that they've been complaining to him. And a lot of other stuff.

—I think Don Goyo is crazy!

—Don't you believe it. I too...

—What?

—A lot of times I've heard the *mangles* talking. When it's flood tide, there's shouting and murmuring everywhere.

Some nights when I've been out in the canoe talking with somebody, the *mangles* mocked me as if they hated me. I told Don Leitón about it. At first I wanted to leave. But then I got used to it.

—That kind of talk scares me.

—But that's why I think Don Goyo is right.

* * *

The moon was hiding behind an enormous black storm cloud. Everything was growing quiet. The *mangle* leaves, touching each other, murmured very softly. Up in the house, the lamplight flickered its waning life. The *cholo* house faded into the dark mass of the hill.

Impulsively, Cusumbo—overwhelmed by ardor— embraced Gertru, kissed her, pressed her against his body. She attempted to pull away:

—Let me go!

—No. I won't let you go. I can't.

He held her even closer. Their lips touched for a long time, like two flames. The *chola* trembled.

—Cusumbo!

He was roaring within. Saw shadows. Felt his nerves tingling as if his flesh were electrified. It had been so long ...

—Gertru!

* * *

He picked her up in his strong arms, and she was willing. He raised his proud head. Climbed over the slippery *ñangas*, scattering the sharp oyster shells, dominating equilibrium and darkness, plunging himself like a knife, with his cherished cargo, into the heart of the brush. He ran.

Jumped like a monkey; as if his powerful feet could adhere to the bark of the *mangles.*

He whispered to her:

—We'll go to the canoe that's hidden under the hammock. Because there nobody will know.

She said nothing. Felt that her will was leaving her, that her thighs were arching in a feverish gesture of unexperienced love, offering herself, that her sex had become a burning coal, that her breasts were harder and more vibrant than the heart of a *cascol* tree.

* * *

They reached the canoe. He let her drop gently to its bottom. Little by little he raised her multicolored skirt. She let her body fall open wantonly in order to make it easier. Then her coarse underclothing, redolent of the inlet's freshness. When his calloused hands surprised her feminine secrets, she trembled.

—Cusumbo!

Then possession. Night held back a furtive cry. The inlet seemed to help them. The canoe made a song of life to the rhythm of the current. Even the wind sang a caress.

There was a pile of clothes on the side. The divine panting of two bodies. Lines of moving shadow. Like a bell tolling life, their two names rocked in the air:

—Gertru.

—Cusumbo.

* * *

When they stopped, Gertru began to weep.

He—still dominant—asked:

—Why are you crying, Gertru?

He tried to kiss her again, to hold her even closer.

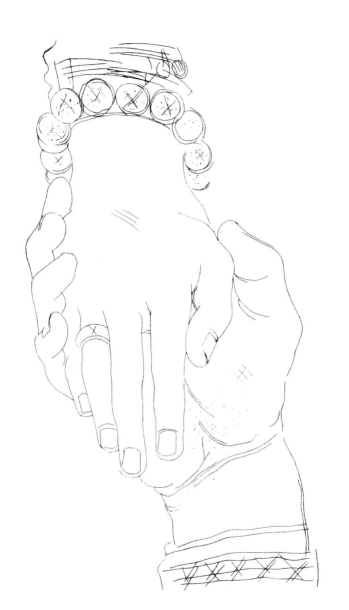

The *chola* firmly pushed him away. Half-standing, she hastily pulled down her skirt.

—Bastard!

—But what's wrong, Gertru?

She looked at him angrily. Then she looked away, at the endless system of estuaries. And sobbed:

—You've screwed me up. Because now we aren't going to cut *mangle* and everything is going wrong for me. This is the start of it. You'll see.

* * *

He passed in front of them. They could barely distinguish him. Don Goyo was going slowly; slowly, as always. The stroke of the oar, slow but firm, had a strange accent as it quietly cut the glittering surface of the water. He looked at nothing. Kept on, slowly, close to the shore, without looking back.

Gertru and Cusumbo looked at each other, full of fear. And—unconsciously—they embraced again, as if to protect each other.

—Gertru!

—Cusumbo!

VI

They made the decision. What else could they do? Don Goyo was like a father to all of them. His voice was always authoritative. His counsel was never disregarded. Besides, he didn't make mistakes. If he didn't want them to cut *mangle*, he must have a reason. In vain they were forcing their minds to try to understand him. The old man was seeing far beyond. And he knew the secrets of all the islands.

And so...

They went out fishing, in Three Mouth Estuary. They were going to try a little harpooning to see if they could catch something big: corvinas, or sea bass, or turtles, or dog sharks, or hammerheads, or yellow jacks.

They were serious and a little sad, rowing furiously, their torsos naked, their muscles taut and feverish, searching the horizon anxiously.

The luminous morning smiled around them. A fresh breeze fanned the water, making it choppy. The *mangles* were greener then ever. It seemed that an overwhelming joy was writhing in their elastic knots. The *cholos* kept on going, faster and faster. Like a sonorous whiplash, the stroke of the oar descended on the ironic spine of the air.

Don Leitón barked:

—Damn the luck that makes me fish for a living. I've forgotten it all. After using the axe and machete...

And somebody else:

—And me also.

—I used to enjoy going after the little ones, the mullet, the needlefish, the devilfish, those horny little blowfish... I liked to stick them with a spear. Grab them. Knew that I could get 'em no matter where they were... But now I'd rather work in the *mangle*. Even though it hurts me to cut them down... I like moving around in those tangled branches. Bitten by the mosquitos. Lashed by the sun and the sea.

* * *

The hunter of leaping fish came alive again in Cusumbo. Little by little the old feeling was taking over. His hand grasped the harpoon nervously. He caressed the length of its shaft all the way up to its steel points.

—Maybe.

Maybe the harpoon would make him enough money to get married, now that he had tried out Gertru and liked her more than ever.

He remembered his years of fishing. First, when he was in the highlands. When he caught *bocachicos* and *biós* from the trees stretched out over the inlets, throwing a trident moored to the branches. Then, when he returned home with the fish, his mother would scale them with a knife, clean them, cutting away their innumerable bones. Then, later, came the years here in the salt estuaries, among the numberless islands, drinking spume and swollen with sun.

He became more and more enthusiastic. Now the *cholos* would see what a man from the highlands could do with a harpoon and a good eye. They would see.

—Could be!

* * *

They reached Three Mouth Inlet. It was a place where the water was as rough as in the open sea. It was so named for the three estuaries that came together there. Two small ones that bordered either side of San Ignacio. The third one large, very large: it was the Chupador Chico that flowed between Chocolate Point and a section of Viña del Mar.

The wind was quite strong, the water very choppy. The canoe had hardly reached the wide part of the estuary when it began jumping. They said that it looked like a big-headed mullet.

—Let's see how it goes!

Cusumbo grasped the harpoon. He stood in the prow. Assumed a beautiful and unconsciously defiant stance, and raised his weapon. His chest inflated, eyes searching, he tried to draw in all the distance.

Abruptly, he let go. The harpoon left his hands swift as a thunderbolt. The *cholos* looked astonished because they hadn't seen a thing.

In a few seconds they heard something paddling a short distance away, conspicuous amidst the heavy waves.

—I got him!

The harpoon lay horizontal on the water, bouyed by its staff of light wood. On the steel end there was a fish, pierced just below the gills, throwing off tiny spirals of blood as he wriggled.

—Don't let him get away!

—Don't worry. He's caught fast. And besides, the harpoon never lets go. The more he fights, the more he's hooked.

The movement of the fish became less violent. Now the harpoon was hardly moving. The canoe approached it rapidly.

They pulled out the resident of the sea. It was a bass. His eyes were still, staring, myopic. He could barely move his tail. The body was destroyed where the harpoon had opened its breach. They pulled him out. Threw him in the bottom of the canoe. And went on.

* * *

Already they had caught several, especially corvinas and sea bass. Cusumbo had served as the harpooner each time. The *cholos* were beginning to show signs of boredom. They were not accustomed to this life. Don Leitón was the first to protest:

—What the hell! This way Cusumbo does all the fishing. And we watching him like fools.

—You're right, Don Leitón!

Another man picked up the harpoon. Cusumbo gave him a little advice. Showed him how to hold the weapon. And he also showed how to throw it so it would fly true.

The new harpooner stood up in the prow of the canoe. Began to scan the horizon. He was anxious, a little nervous. Several moments passed. The canoe continued moving forward rapidly and he still had not thrown the harpoon even once. Bored, he commented:

—I don't see a thing!

Then Cusumbo stood up. He went over to him. Extending his arm, he pointed:

—See that tiny blade going toward the *ñanga?* That's a bass. Look at him travel!

The other man tried to see it. He cast his eyes like a fish hook across the wrinkled surface of the water. He could distinguish nothing.

—Where?

Cusumbo took the harpoon again. He extended it, indicating with its point:

—There!

—Right. Now I see it!

He took the harpoon from Cusumbo. Raised it. Threw it hard. But his lack of skill made him miss. The lance skipped twice on the water. And fell near the canoe.

—Damn it all!

The fish seemed to be mocking him. It came near the canoe. Briefly submerged. And then appeared again, cutting sharp angles in the estuary water. Possibly chasing a school of small mullet or *chaparras.*

Cusumbo laughed:

—It's all in knowing how!

And then he grasped the harpoon again. Turned and arched himself in a powerful stance. Grasped the nimble weapon more and more firmly. As if he were sewing—with a giant needle—he made definitive stitches in the multi-colored cloth of the water.

* * *

They were returning. Not bad for the first day. Rowing lazily. The sun burning their magnificent backs. A great number of fish were still writhing in the bottom of the canoe because many of them had barely been caught by the tail. But what Cusumbo had said was true. The harpoon granted no pardons. Once a fish was caught on its strong hooks, it was captive. No matter how much it protested, how much it wriggled, how much it tried to escape. And the old blood of the *mangles* that tanned the gunwales seemed to blend with the new blood of dying fish.

The canoe was moving slowly. Now the mullet jumped—from time to time—close to them, as if challenging them. The silver of their swift scales was constantly flashing.

—If we'd brought the casting net...

—Right.

—But it doesn't matter. These nights are dark. And it's best to go at night. We can cast the net better. And catch a lot of fish.

—Well, let's go out tonight.

—No. Tomorrow. We're very tired now.

—All right.

The top of Cerrito de los Morreños seemed to rear up to see them coming.

* * *

The time came to send them to Guayas. Don Leitón said:

—We need to deliver this load early.

—It's not much of a load!

—That doesn't matter. Something's better than nothing. We've got to buy bananas, rice, salt, and lard...if we can find them.

—In that case...

—Who wants to go?

Nobody moved.

Then Don Leitón resigned himself:

—All right then. I'll go myself, with two of you boys.

Cusumbo intervened:

—Why don't we salt 'em down and wait till we have more.

—We need food supplies. You know that. This is the last trip of the "Mercedes Orgelina." If there's no *mangle* there's no reason for her to make the trip. And you can't live and work without eating.

—That's true.

—That's the way...

—It makes sense.

VII

That night everything was fish. Fish in the stew. Fish in the rice. Fish with the fried banana. Fish, pure fish. Each one of the *cholos* swallowed some fish, as much as he could. The house, with its one large room, took on a penetrating odor that cut the air like a whip. The *cholos* were sitting on the cane floor, on crates that had once contained cans of kerosene. Cusumbo, sitting by Gertru, spoke very slowly:

—Listen, Gertru.

—What?

—You want to go out with me tonight?

—Go where?

—For a ride in the canoe. We'll cast nets. I told the others we'd go tomorrow; but that was because I wanted to go by myself.

—I see. Well go by yourself, as you said. I don't want you messing with me again.

—But, Gertru...

—No. That's final.

—All right, then.

He was taking huge swallows of fisherman's coffee from a chipped enamel cup. Eating a banana dumpling with it. And he remembered, remembered when Gertru had served him the black liquid for the first time.

* * *

He got up. Went down from the house. Walked rapidly to the shore. He boarded the canoe and started rowing. It was fairly dark already. Things were beginning to blur their outlines in this hour of dark gray. Everything had become silent, and had taken on the stillness of death.

Abruptly he heard a shout from the bank:

—Cusumbo! Cusumbo!

He turned around slowly:

—What's going on?

—Wait a minute for me.

—All right, then.

It was just as he had always said: you have to treat women rough to make them gentle and obedient. If he had hung around, begging, they probably wouldn't have gone out together that night. Ah, women!

He veered and brought the canoe in coolly. Gertru was waiting impatiently. As soon as he got there, she blurted:

—Where are you going?

—To El Empalado.

—Oh. Would you like me to go with you?

—Yes, if you want to. Since you're so hard up for company.

—You see? It's just like I said ... If you let them try the fruit, they may not buy the fruit. You're tired of me already. Isn't that true?

—That's not true. If it had been, I wouldn't have invited you today.

—All right. Take me with you in that case.

—Let's go then.

Gertru sat in the stern and began to steer the canoe. Cusumbo was in the bow, watching for the schools of mullet, ready to cast out the fatal arm of his net.

A slight wind was coming up. The estuary was growing choppy. Night was closing in over the islands, rapid and bold.

—Soon we'll see the mullet!

He readied the net—made of strong cord and massive lead sinkers. He held one end in his mouth. And stretched his hands to open it, like a large bell.

With his inquisitive eyes, he began to probe the darkness, making taut his ears and nose, just in case ...

Suddenly he murmured:

—Shh!

Gertru held the oar still. The canoe began to move slowly. Cusumbo grew even more attentive. They heard the almost imperceptible sound of breaking water. He detected the serpentine flash of a school of mullet like the flight of an arrow.

—Here they are!

He balanced the casting net swiftly. Threw it. The cords' embrace fell in a large circle, covering the spot. The lead closed up the net rapidly. Many fish were jumping around in the sack.

—Look, I caught some!

With difficulty, he pulled up on the mullet trap. Spume was gushing. In the darkness, they saw the shiny scales glittering in the tortuous mass of cords.

—Look, I caught some!

Slowly, he loosened the various pouches of the net. The fish were falling, falling into the bottom of the canoe or jumping over the sides.

Gertru—in the shadow—tried to imagine the muscles of the *montuvio*-become-*cholo*. And she rowed and rowed.

* * *

They had pulled in the canoe peppered with fish that were still alive, jumping, bumping against the sides of the boat, constantly dilating their gills, striking the gunwales.

Cusumbo proposed:

—Let's cook a few.

—Good idea.

Gertru went to the inevitable grill in the center of the canoe, in which a termite nest was still smoking weakly. She stirred it up with some chips. Put on the iron bars. And threw some mullet that were still wriggling on the fire without opening them, without washing them.

—That way they don't lose their flavor.

The rich odor of broiled mullet filled the air. In the bottom of the canoe, the remaining fish seemed to stare myopically. Gertru and Cusumbo relished the smell for a while. After some time, the mullet were ready. In the dim light of the tiny flames they looked like gold.

—They're nice and fat!

Each one took a fish. Opened it, peeling it like a banana. Cleaned it. Attacked it with sharp, strong teeth.

They started back.

*　*　*

When they were almost there, at a turn in the estuary where it was even darker, Cusumbo couldn't hold back and murmured very softly:

—Gertru?

—What?

—Once more ... want to?

The *chola* protested. Gestured impatiently:

—We always get back to that! No! Leave me alone!

—All right, then.

He stretched out full length in the canoe. Let the current sweep them along. A strange anger was taking control of him. Then Gertru spoke:

—Are you sleeping, Cusumbo?

—No.

—Well what's wrong with you?

—Nothing.

—Then why are you so quiet?

—I didn't know I was so quiet!

Gertru got up. Went over to him. Stared at him steadily for a long time. And spit out these words:

—What's wrong is what I've always told you: "If you let them try the fruit..."

Cusumbo sat up.

—No. That's not it. You know what it is? What's wrong is that you have to treat women rough, as if they were mules. That's the only way they're happy. The only way they'll let a man do what he wants. Treating them nice doesn't amount to anything. You have to throw 'em down in the *mangle* groves... or anywhere. And then get on top of 'em. That's why you're acting so fancy.

—That's not so!

—That's what you say!

She got up. Went to the stern. Started rowing again. Rowed furiously. The canoe leapt forward, like a mullet, like an enormous, big-headed mullet. It swallowed the distances. Threw a full beard of spume. The enormous *pechiche* canoe.

VIII

The men who took the fish to Guayaquil got back at dawn. Even at that hour almost everybody was awake to greet them. They asked for two lamps. Ña Andrea got up and started making coffee and frying green bananas. The newcomers sat down in the middle of the room and old man Leitón recited the vicissitudes of the journey:

—We've been having bad luck. From the minute we left, everything went wrong. First thing, here, in the inlet, we couldn't get past El Cruce because the water was so rough we couldn't make headway. And so we got to Guayas late and wet.

The *cholos* listened attentively. Down below, the waters of the estuary seemed to protest, throwing themselves violently against the shore. From San Ignacio, on the wings of the wind, came the cry of a bird: Boo-hoo-loo-hoo-ree-ooo. The tiny flames of the lamps seemed to want to gutter out, as if they were sleepy. Don Leitón continued:

—Since we arrived late, nobody wanted to buy the fish.

Above all, if you want to sell your fish, you need to have an agreement with one of the White Men who buy and sell in the city. So we were screwed. We got tired of waiting for somebody to offer us a price for the lot. So we picked out the best ones and started out to peddle them ourselves. But we didn't know anybody, so we couldn't sell many. And we couldn't carry but one string in each hand...

The coffee began to smell good. They heard the crackling of the burning wood. Ña Andrea flitted about:

—That's the way it is!

Don Leitón continued:

—To make a long story short: When we went back to the canoe, where we had left a man to take care of the fish, we found they had been neglected and were already smelling bad. And we had to throw them in the water. We went downtown to buy a little salt, rice, and lard. With only what little money we had! I didn't even get to pour a drink. Damn it all!

* * *

Lost in the shadows, the *cholos* were whispering:

—Me without bananas!

—And me!

—And me!

—I can do without anything but bananas. That really screws me up!

—And me!

—It's Don Goyo's fault. If it weren't for him, we'd be in good shape now.

—He's changed. Don't you think so?

—Who knows! When he acts like that...

—Damn it. And now what're we going to do? This fishing is good for nothing.

—And the worst thing is that we don't know a damn thing about it.

—We better catch something. Catch crabs, mussels, crayfish, oysters. Who knows what?

—Damn it all! You never know what a man will have to do. Right?

—Right.

—Well, and what about Don Goyo? He's not back yet.

Don Leitón, who heard the last remark, murmured:

—I think Don Goyo's been talking with Old Nick.

—Maybe so.

—All this stuff makes me feel bad. What's it going to amount to? Me, I'd rather cut *mangle*.

—Don Goyo doesn't want it. And he must have a good reason!

—Damn it!

* * *

Without warning, when they were least prepared, Don Goyo appeared—serene, tranquil, a strange smile on his lips, walking slowly, slightly bent over, looking around him:

—God grant you a good day.

—Good day, Don Goyo.

They looked at him astonished, as if they were seeing a ghost. Then they lowered their heads, waiting in complete silence. From near the brazier arose Ña Andrea's voice:

—Coffee's ready.

Don Goyo turned around.

—Good. Pour it.

And then, looking steadily at the *cholos*, he murmured:

—And you, what's wrong with you that you look

astonished to see me? You'd think I was a ghost. Tell me what's going on.

—Nothing. Just that the men who went to Guayas could sell nothing because they got there late and the fish had to be left on the beach.

Don Goyo looked thoughtful. Even more wrinkles appeared in the forest of wrinkles on his face.

—Damn, that's bad news!

Ña Andrea came over with the coffee cups in her hand and began to serve them all. It commenced slowly to grow light. From the canopy of nets hanging against the wall came fitful breathing. An occasional snore and the whine of a circling mosquito looking for a hole in the net.

Don Leitón, making an effort, ventured:

—Look, Don Goyo...It's about...

—About what?

—About you, and the *mangles*, and fishing, and all of us...

—All right, what about it?

Don Leitón was somewhat embarassed. He stopped a minute, hesitating, not sure what to say. He looked at the *cholos* around him and, taking courage because of them, continued:

—Well,...we're no good at fishing. We don't have a knack for launching the harpoons or the spears or throwing the casting nets, or the spiking nets and we don't even have a knack for selling fish. A man's got to be what he was born to be, Don Goyo. And we've got *manglero* blood.

—All right. And what else?

—We want to go back to cutting *mangle*, Don Goyo. We can't fish. Everything goes wrong. You see how it is...Even Gertru's and Cusumbo's wedding...You can't be without money...You know how it is, Don Goyo.

Don Goyo had been listening attentively. When he stopped talking, Don Goyo went over to him, almost touched him. He half straightened his permanently bent body. And he spoke:

—You don't act like men!

Don Leitón protested:

—Don Goyo!

The old man silenced him with a glance. He trembled slightly. Insisted:

—You don't act like men... At the first sign of trouble, you give up... As if you couldn't find a thousand ways to make a living, without hurting anything else... So what if you can't fish?... Then try shellfishing. Catch oysters, or clams or *pata de mula* or shrimp, or crabs, or mussels, or anything else, or make some salt beds, or work as a diver. *Mangle* is not the only way to make a living... You don't act like men... You've tried only one thing... And right away you say "We can't. We can't... We were born to cut *mangle*"... Cowards!

Don Leitón had turned ashen. He spoke violently, as if an inlet in flood tide had made lumps in his throat:

—All right, Don Goyo. We will go shellfishing. But it's the last thing. If it doesn't work out, we're going back to *mangle*. Anyway, I am.

—All of us.

—All right.

*   *   *

Dawn was breaking already. Slowly it began to clear along the shore. Little by little women were raising their sleeping nets and going outside. The *cholos* were still talking in little groups, between Don Goyo and Don Leitón. A light breeze stirred the air. They heard—from the direction of San Ignacio—the sound of the whole forest waking.

IX

They went out shellfishing very early. First they were
going to catch "shellcrackers" among the *mangle* roots,
when the tide was at its lowest and they all floated on the
mud left behind. They rowed slowly as if they were lazy or
unwilling. They traveled in two canoes talking of better
times, remembering their lives as cutters of *mangle,* as
choppers of wood, or of the dried bark so precious in
tanning. The sun macheted their shining backs. The canoes
slithered along without making the slightest noise.

Cusumbo spoke:

—I wonder if we're going to get as rusty as our axes.
Since we stopped cutting *mangle,* they're getting as brown as
the earth. Maybe they won't even take an edge again.

—Maybe. The only thing I hate is to sleep the whole
blessed day, without doing anything. Or maybe screwing my
woman . . . I'm as dull as my axe. Damn it!

They stopped talking. Looked at the line of *mangles*
that were standing tall and slim, pluming all the shore.
Their eyes followed the trees. Examined them caressingly.
They hunted for the easiest places to cut, the side where they
would fall best. Then they could trim them, and leave them
in logs or split them. And soon realizing that it could not be,
that they were daydreaming, a strange sorrow came over
them. They lowered their heads and murmured, all of them
this time:

—Damn it all!

* * *

They drove a stake reaching well above the film of mud
that spread over the tranquil water like an immense sheet.

They tied up the canoe, and then sinking up to their knees, began climbing up the *mangles.*

As they stepped on the first hanging roots, they felt strange. It seemed like a long time, a very long time, since they had been there. It was as if they were dealing with a totally unknown element. They were afraid of slipping and cutting their very souls on the sharp oyster shells. Half-trembling, they climbed into the closest *ñangas,* scaring away the snails and water spiders that were living in the tangled branches.

—Let's see...

They spread out, walking with difficulty on the *ñangas,* forced to hold onto the branches with their hands, their spirits hungering and their eyes watchful.

The "shellcrackers" poked through the top of the mud from time to time, in the middle of a dense net of the innumerable hanging roots. They blended into the predominantly gray color of the roots, branches, and mud. The ones that could be seen most easily were the *lloronas*— the "weepers"—that are white, and that in some manner make a discordant note in the uniform gray ambience.

However, they found only a few—either because of their inexperience, or because the *cholo* fishermen who worked that area had caught most of them already.

Meanwhile, the *cholos* kept on complaining:

—Damn it...

—What's wrong?

—What now! An oyster has gotten me! And me with feet like leather! I don't know what's happening in this place. Damn it all!

—And I've fallen down three times. They must have greased these things with shit! And even the mosquitos are biting me as never before. I don't know what we're going to do, but this is unbearable!

—Right!

* * *

Each one of the men had been depositing the "conchcrackers" he caught in a gunny sack. After about three hours of this work, the men on the shore began yelling in protest.

Gradually they began to emerge one by one from the tangled net of the thick *mangles*. They were breathing hard, red faced, covered with welts that had been caused by the mosquitoes. They walked with difficulty, carrying sacks of gasping shell fish on their backs. When they were all together, they looked at each other silently. They walked directly to the shore.

The tide had risen a bit. The canoe had been left half aground, but now it was afloat and the murmuring water of the estuary was making it tug at its mooring. In order to get aboard, the *cholos* had to plunge into the water and half pull the canoe toward them.

They emptied their sacks. And could barely hold back their rage. They had caught almost nothing. The few "conchcrackers" they had taken were small ones. Pure junk. Not even worth carrying to market.

—Well, then... when the tide's half in, we'll try oystering. Let's try Los Colorados inlet, where I think fewest people go. Because with this we're doing wretchedly. We don't have enough to make a good rice and shell soup.

—Let's go.

—I think what's happening to us is that we're in a streak

of bad luck. Maybe a badger pissed on us. Or anyway, on Don
Goyo.

—Don Goyo!

They left La Seca inlet. Began to row furiously. The
canoe leapt ahead in the rhythm of a savage trot. Don Leitón
murmured.

—We have to hurry because the water is rising fast. If we
don't get there soon, the oysters will be too deep and we
won't get any.

They stirred up the termite nest fire, which could really
be helpful to them now because they wouldn't have to go
into the *mangle*, but could carry on their oystering from the
canoe.

*   *   *

In a little while they reached Los Colorados Inlet, which
is right at San Ignacio Island. They went in slowly and
explored all the *mangle* roots to see where the oysters were.

Cusumbo—with the experience of a fisherman—said
quietly:

—We have to go further in. Here at the mouth the
fishermen have already cleaned them up. Only the small
ones are left. They're no good at all. Let's go further in.

In the *ñanga* thickets, on the twisted *mangle* trunks, on
the bending limbs, on the endless mass of branches, the
oysters clustered, whitening the dividing line between the
water and the *mangle* leaves.

As they approached the estuary's source, the oysters were
in fact much larger. They clustered there in smaller
numbers. Many branches doubled with their weight.

—These are good ones. We can start.

—Let's start.

They put in to the shore. Began to inch along. Cusumbo went to the prow. He caught a limb that was sticking out over the inlet and pulled the canoe in under it. Then, with the back of his machete, he started hitting the clump of oysters. They fell into the canoe a few at a time. After leaving that limb completely clean, they went on. When there was a good bunch hanging on a slim *ñanga* root, they cut off the whole thing and put it in the canoe.

Quickly they filled the canoe so full it was hardly riding above the water. Then they started back home.

The flood tide had begun to submerge most of the hanging branches. Now the only ones above water were floating high in the air and full of leaves that painted large definitive green brush strokes over the arched neck of the islands.

* * *

Just to check, they started opening some oysters, suffering a disappointment. In spite of their appearance, they were still too small. Don Leitón, wise in the ways of the Guayas market, spoke pessimistically:

—We're going to have trouble getting a good price for these. They're too small. They bring rock oysters from lots of places to Guayas—from Puntilla, San Miguel, El Guaybo. And the rock oysters are lots bigger than these, with shells like serving trays. The hucksters are going to want to pay us about half ... We've wasted another morning.

—Damn it.

His blood was beginning to boil. Cusumbo said nothing; but sometimes he felt as if someone had placed a black curtain over his eyes.

But what was Don Goyo thinking about? Did he figure

they were willing to keep on getting screwed just because he had fancied that they ought not to cut *mangle?* He was wrong. That afternoon they'd try one more time. If not . . . It was god's will . . . And if they didn't have any luck . . . Well, they'd see . . . They were tired of working for the fun of it.

—Damn it all!

*   *   *

That afternoon they went to catch mussels, to catch crabs, to catch crayfish and "mules' hooves": anything they could. They split up into several groups. And when the tide was low enough, each group went out in a canoe to the neighboring islands.

The first ones stayed close by, right in front of El Cerrito. And started crabbing.

—It scares me.

—What's that?

—That one of these bastards is going to grab me with its claw.

—You got to know how. You put your hand in the hole and catch him. Because these animals go into their holes with their claws crossed.

—We'll see.

There were countless holes among the *ñanga* thickets. From time to time, a crab, protected by his hard shell, crawled around among the hanging roots. But as soon as he sensed the presence of humans, he tried to escape. The *cholos* contemplated them calmly:

—If only we'd brought a little harpoon.

—It wouldn't do any good because these animals evaporate whenever anything touches them.

—But they can use their claws!

—That's all they can use!

They had tied up the few they caught with some cord they had brought along. They were hard at work when someone yelled:

—Sonofabitch!

Everybody turned toward him.

—What's wrong man?

The *cholo* held up his hand, pulling it out with a jerk from the hole where he had stuck it. And then, astonished, they all saw an enormous blue-shelled crustacean hanging from it. Thick drops of blood fell to the ground. They half realized that a toothed pincer had closed onto one of the poor man's fingers.

—It's a *sin boca*!

The *cholo*, making a desperate effort, slammed the animal against a *mangle* limb. The crustacean jerked clumsily a few seconds. And then it stopped moving, hung rigid, its feet spread apart, but without releasing the bitten finger; and it kept on hanging from the *cholo's* flesh; bathed in blood, with its eyes extended like two small periscopes.

—I'm screwed!

It took considerable effort to separate the pincers of the crustacean. It seemed as if they had been permanently soldered. When they finally got them loose, they could see that the *cholo's* finger was filled with a double line of holes. Then they all began trembling:

—I'm telling you, I've caught my last crab. As far as I'm concerned, the whole bunch can die of starvation. But I'm not going to let one of those devils screw me.

—Me neither.

They loaded the little they had caught in the canoe. And set out toward El Cerrito.

* * *

The men who went to catch mussels had better luck. But mussels are very delicate and, besides, you can't go to the same place over and over. Because once a beach is cleaned out, it stays that way. Of course, you may even catch some *michullas,* and perhaps some clams at the same time.

The *cholos,* accompanied by Cusumbo, had been watching for the *rayito* shells, that push up the sandy mud slightly, making it look like a woman's pubis. As soon as they saw one, they would go after it, machete in hand, and dig out the grasping shellfish.

—Careful, don't let him get away.

—Get away?

—Yeah. The mussels slide over the sand. Dig their way down to the bottom of the mud, and then nobody can find them.

—You're wrong.

The *michullas* are the ones that go through the sand. You've heard the rooster crow, but you don't know where.

Cusumbo intervened:

—That's right. The *michullas* travel through the sand, making a tunnel as they go.

* * *

As for *pata-de-mulas,* not a sign of one. It seemed that the earth had swallowed them. No matter how much they dove, no matter how much they probed the shoals with their oars, they couldn't find any. They were able to catch only a few crabs. Since the tide was already rising and the estuary was getting choppy, they had to get back to El Cerrito, bald-pated El Cerrito de los Morreños.

X

All the *cholos* were sitting on the bank, below the houses of El Cerrito that seemed pasted against the hillside. Most of them were sitting on *mangle* trunks cut for the port, or on the rafts used for mooring canoes when they were in the water. The men were silent, taciturn, uncertain what they ought to do. Suddenly Don Leitón stood up.

—I can't stand it, I feel my blood boiling. We don't have anything to eat. Who knows what will happen to us if the "Mercedes Orgelina" doesn't bring us something?

—And when do you think she'll arrive, Don Leitón?

—Maybe tomorrow. She ought to be on the way here now.

—We'll see.

The inlet came up almost to their feet and there gently died down. It seemed to smile. The *mangles* were peopled by the murmuring of the *ñangas'* endless rosary.

Don Leitón spoke again:

—Once I was a fisherman. I loved to cast the net, to go and hunt at night for the fish poisoned by mullein, to pick them out still half alive. But one night it seemed that all the fish were looking right at me. With their eyes that inspired pity, peace, sadness, as if they were pleading with me. It gave me chills. I began to run through the mud. I embarked in my canoe as quickly as I could. And I've been afraid to fish ever since. Until Cusumbo asked me to come down here. And then I left my fishing nets forever. And I began to swing the ax, the best I could..."

They interrupted him:

—Just what do you expect us to get from all that, Don Leitón?

—That I believe it's worse to kill fish than to cut

mangle, if the Old Man was to take pity on something.
—You're right.

* * *

Suddenly someone murmured:
—Hey, what happened to Cusumbo?
—Yeah, where is he?
They started looking for him. Went up to the houses, one by one, asking everyone if they had seen Cusumbo. At Ña Andrea's house, another piece of news surprised them. Neither was Gertru there.
—Have they run away?
They flew down. Made for the shore. Counted the canoes. They were all there.
—No. They haven't run away. Around here nobody's going anywhere by land.
—Then I know. Cusumbo is gettin' that stuff. They're probably behind the thicket at El Cruce.
—Let's go see!
—Let's go!
They began to walk rapidly, with a sensuous curiosity that made their lips and nostrils tremble slightly, their sharp gimlet eyes penetrating the dark.

* * *

They were indeed behind the thicket. They hadn't noticed anybody coming. Holding their breath and well-hidden behind some yuccas, and rocks, the *cholos* could watch them.
They saw the lovers completely naked, at the height of possession. They moved urgently. Their excited bodies panted with anxiety. Their voices stammered.

—Gertru!
—Cusumbo!
—I'm going back to cutting *mangle*, Gertru.
—G-o-o-ood...
—So we can g-e-et married soo-oon...
—Yes...
—And be-e-e together all-l-l-ways!
The *cholos* could sense their relief, their relaxation, their tranquility. Both bodies had grown still. Cusumbo was stretched out by her side caressing her.

* * *

Don Leitón said:
—Let's stop them.
—No. It's too late. Why should we say anything to them? He's already layed her. Now let 'em get married. That's what people are meant to do.
They felt envious. Most of the *cholos*, even the old, married men, felt envious. What a fine woman that Gertru was!

PART THREE

DON GOYO

I

—There she comes!

Rounding Chocolate Point, the sloop hove into view—the long awaited "Mercedes Orgelina." Her triangular sails were outlined, graceful and majestic, against a pure blue sky. A strong wind from the north filled the mainsail, the foresail, the jib. They must have had a steady wind blowing because her stern was closing in and they had also run the gaffsail up the topmast. She was coming in fast. They could already distinguish her necklace of foam, her green belly black with pitch at the water line, and her vibrant red rigging conspicuous against the surface of the estuaries.

They could see the *cholo* pilot, completely serene, grasping the spokes of the helm, anticipating the arrival. Two sailors were near the sails, ready to obey the captain's orders.

—The "Orgelina" is really loaded down.

—Looks that way!

The waves swelled. The sloop could be made out perfectly in its least detail. Her strong, blunt prow continued to cut through the water, faster and faster.

—They ought to be bringing in a real load of bananas, with the *mangle* they took out.

—They ought to be!

—If they aren't, we're screwed. I think we've even run out of salt around here!

*   *   *

They could hear the pilot shouting:

—Haul in the mainsail!

The two sailors were slackening the sail little by little, first one side then the other. For his part, the pilot had also begun to take hold of the gaffsail boom bringing it round to center. And then taking care that the spar came down within the topping lifts.

The sloop diminished its velocity. She was already near Cerrito. Men and women from all the houses had come down to welcome the ship.

—Haul in the foresail!

This time, because they were so close, they clearly heard the tielines paying out. Above, one sailor had to handle the line as it slackened. The sloop almost stopped, helped in its movement now only by the jibsail.

They heard, at last, the command:

—Drop anchor!

The two sailors went forward to the prow. And they removed the steel chain that was holding the links together. The chain spent out rapidly and with great force. The anchor, on reaching bottom, stopped the sloop, with a shudder.

* * *

—Let's go aboard!

—Let's go!

They set out in several canoes. Rowed furiously. In a few seconds they covered the distance separating them from the sloop.

—God grant you a good day!

—Good day!

—How've things been going?

—So so . . . nothing special.

—Well . . .

—And here?

—Same as usual. Everything the same.

They climbed aboard nimbly. Walked around the deck. Shook hands with the two sailors. Then jumped down into the hold. And immediately started unloading.

A delicious odor of fresh banana came up from the belly of the sloop. And, indeed, numerous stalks of this exquisite bread of the tropics stood up to be greeted by the sun. They also noticed that there were many sacks of who knows what.

—Did you bring some *barragano* bananas? Or are they all *dominicos*?

—We brought some *barraganos*.

—That's good. It's the kind I like best.

The provisions were brought up on deck and then loaded into the canoes. In a very short time the sloop was completely unloaded.

The pilot went over to Don Leitón.

—What's happened to all you people? I've been noticing something strange ever since I got here. What's been going on here lately? Spit it out, Don Leitón!

Don Leitón hesitated a moment; but finally made up his mind:

—Sooner or later you're going to find out. So I may as well be the one to tell you. What's happening is this: it appears that Don Goyo has lost his senses, and he's gotten it into his head that the oldest *mangle* tree in these parts, according to him, spoke to him the other day and asked him not to cut any more *mangle*. We've had to start fishing and crabbing. And since we don't know . . .

—That's a helluva note . . . So there's no cargo for the sloop. Right?

—Nothing to eat either. We're screwed.

—Hell! And where do you suppose the Old Man got that idea?

—Who knows. Maybe he had a session with Old Nick.

—Maybe. But for my part, I'm going to keep on cutting *mangle*. Nobody's going to make my children starve. I've got to have work for my sloop. If I don't, what did I build her for?

—You're right, Captain Lino.

—And you men ought to do the same. The Old Man is getting along. You can't do everything he says.

—Yes, but the fellows love and respect him too much. And so they are just obeying him.

—That's a bad situation.

* * *

They jumped ashore. Everybody greeted the pilot enthusiastically.

—How are you, Captain Lino?

—How did you do over in Guayas?

—So, so. Same as usual.

They went up to Ña Andrea's house. Seeing there was no fire in the ovens, he asked:

—Well, isn't there anything to eat yet?

—No, Captain.

—And why not?

—Because we don't have anything to cook.

Captain Lino frowned and went over to sit down on a small trunk that stood in the corner.

—I brought in supplies of all kinds. Pick out something and cook it; I'm hungry.

—We're all hungry!

The *cholos* silently gathered around Captain Lino and Don Leitón. They hung on their words, hoping one of them would come up with a solution to the problem that lay so heavily on them. Finally, Captain Lino spoke:

—Well, boys. It's necessary to work this out. I'll keep on working the *mangle*, as always. It's the only thing I'm good

for. It's what I've been doing all my life, besides caulking
canoes and building sloops. So anybody who wants can
come and work with me. And anybody who doesn't can
continue with Don Goyo. It's a question of every man
deciding for himself.

Don Leitón interrupted:

—I want to propose something. The best thing would
be to make Don Goyo change his mind and then all of us
could keep cutting *mangle*.

—And if he won't change it?

—Then we'll go ahead ourselves. And do what we want.

—If that's so... When are we going to tell him?

—This very night.

—All right. It's best!

II

All of them—men and women—surrounded him. Little
by little they closed in like an enormous human casting net,
in silence, tremulously, with their eyes downcast, without
uttering a syllable. Don Goyo—whom they found sitting on
an empty kerosene crate—stood up. He looked around him,
and spoke with authority:

—Say what it is you want!

Don Leitón stepped forward hesitatingly.

—Speak up!

The circle of *cholos* drew in even closer. Don Goyo
looked at them, astonished, not knowing what to do. He
repeated:

—Speak up!

Then Don Leitón murmured timidly:

—We don't know how to fish. It's not for us. In the last few days we've gotten more screwed up than ever. We're not going to have food to eat. And besides... we're coming to hate this crazy life of catching fish. We can't fish.

—Good, don't fish!

—It's that...

—What?

—We want to go back to the *mangle*. It's the one thing that we know. And it's the only way we can earn a living. And we're going to return, Don Goyo, tomorrow morning...

Don Goyo was disgusted. His blood ran foaming through his veins, like a great wave. He roared:

—All right!

Don Leitón tried to explain:

—It's the only way. We can't all fuck ourselves up at once. We're no good for fishing or for anything except the *mangle*. We were born with axes in our hands. It's the only way!

There, in the distance, they saw a tangled mass of *mangles* rear up. The estuary twisted like a quicksilver snake. The axes laughed in their corners. Don Leitón kept turning over the same monotonous phrases:

—It can't be, Don Goyo. We've tried to do something else. But haven't gotten anywhere. We're no good for anything but the axe. If we don't use it, we'll all just go from bad to worse.

And anyway, couldn't he have been mistaken the other night? Couldn't that conversation with the *mangle* have been a dream? Wasn't it maybe the devil's trick? Especially in times like these, when christian people generally had turned to evil! Anybody could be deceived. Even God himself...

*   *   *

Don Goyo remained still a moment, pensive, meticulously searching deep within for his words. He looked out the window briefly. The inlet, the distant islands, the endless vegetation on their silent shores. The *cholos* continued their moving, full of fear. Finally, he decided:

—All right...cut *mangle*...do what you want. But don't count on me any longer...As for me, I'll never cut *mangle* again...I'll be able to live some way...maybe even hunting every day...

He was growing excited. His voice fell, harsh and penetrating, like a harpoon upon the inclined bodies of his listeners...

—You people are good for nothing...The White Man will order you around forever...And one day nobody will be able to live in these parts. And then you'll remember old Don Goyo...Cut *mangle*...Do anything you want to do.

The *cholos* were slowly leaving. Nobody said a single word. They sought out the corners, and began to murmur.

Don Goyo walked over to the window, his step slow and uncertain. And through it he was able to see the tiny world that had framed his entire life.

* * *

He was remembering.

He had come to these islands more than a hundred years ago. Come from San Miguel de Morro. And because of this he gave the name Cerrito de los Morreños to the piece of high ground where he settled down.

When he came, there was nobody else in the region. The islands, virgin and solitary, demonstrated their hostility. Before all of his initiatives they always had the resistance of a wall, as if they were defending their inviolability, undesecrated, to the very last. Several times he was on the point of giving up. But his urge to struggle and to triumph made him continue, always continue, trying to break down, to destroy definitively the innumerable obstacles encountered on his path, as if he had been transformed into an auger of human flesh that could penetrate the heart of the islands and the *mangle*.

He had come there in a tiny canoe, his only weapon a sharp machete; then he had cut a few forks of knotty *mangle* and some timbers from the palms. He drove them into the fertile earth, near the hill on the bank of the inlet. And built his first *rancho*, with no walls and no roof, poorly covered with the fallen leaves he had managed to collect with difficulty, in the inclement weather, as they swirled perpetually in the wind that licked constantly at the inlet's surface.

Although he might not have preferred it, he had to become *macho. Macho* in everything. In his solitude, he forgot his specters. He had no fear of death, or of ghosts, or of the Devil himself. Sun and water fell daily on his body as if falling on unfeeling stone. He stepped on thorns, walked on oyster shells, clung with the soles of his feet to the slippery backs of mud-covered piles of branches. The mosquitoes, the gnats hung like a cloud over all his body. He didn't even notice them. He felt he was changing, changing completely. When he saw his reflection in the water, when he undressed completely and passed his hand over all his body, he noted differences. He imagined tumultuous flesh twisting beneath the shining skin. He found a certain pleasant similarity to the strongest wood of the region. And little by little a sense of power, of strength, of invincibility saturated the length and breadth of his spirit.

* * *

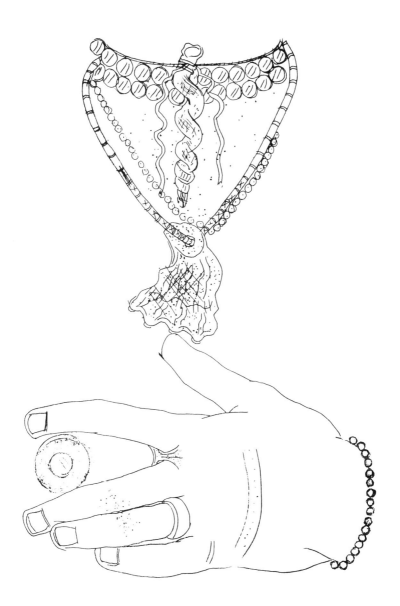

Suddenly the islands delivered themselves. Were surrendering like lascivious women. They tried to make amends to the man who had struggled with them for so long, and had finally conquered because of his faith and tenacity. Gradually they began to reveal themselves as they really were. They guided him, with his intangible desires, into their most secret places. They rewarded all his efforts. They came to love him, in this awakening of millenial dreams. Marine treasures seemed to spring up and float on the water among the tangled, sunken *ñanga* roots. Everything became clear and easy. He, solitary, ceased being lonely. These surroundings, once hostile and strange, took care of him, watched over him, told him a thousand things, gave him much advice, as no friend had ever done before.

Don Goyo rowed his triumphal canoe through the interminable estuaries. He forgot the rest of humanity, forgot San Miguel del Morro, forgot all that had gone before. His first thirty years, dull and cloudy, mysteriously vanished from his memory. He had desire and strength only for living in the present. For continuing the struggle that seemed now to be growing easy and agreeable.

Every morning he went out to fish, or to gather oysters, or shrimp, or crabs. In the afternoon, he chopped wood. Enough to go to Guayas every month and get the rest of the food he needed, and very rarely, to purchase himself a shirt or a new pair of pants. He went to bed very early. Fell like a stone. He never dreamed. Had no ambitions of any kind. He lived a monotonous, calm, drab life without ups and downs and with a health of body and soul that maintained him in enviable and constant equilibrium.

He resolved his sexual problems in Guayas, on one of the rafts very near where he tied up his canoe. Took any of those women called *peseteras*, the cheapest kind. And he cast the stone three or four times, as the saying goes.

Little by little he had improved his house. Had gathered wild canepoles. Had split them, removing the knots within. And then, he had nailed them one by one to the wall timbers. He did the same thing with the roof. And, insofar as he could, he covered them with broad *bijao* leaves. He had also bought himself a beautiful heavy axe with which he felt capable of cutting all the *mangle* groves on the islands. He had also constructed a casting net of strong, twisted cord with which he would go out to fish now and then. These things, along with a few hooks, a harpoon, and a gig, constituted, for the time, all he had.

* * *

A wave of excitement seemed to run along the gulf coast. Some said that over there, on the other side of the Guayas peninsula, there was a virgin archipelago favorable for working, rich in wood, in fish and shellfish, accessible for the most part, that had been waiting for a long time for the tread of men.

And it was like telling the beads of a rosary. New settlers came from different places. They arrived in canoes and on rafts, full of enthusiasm, able to struggle and conquer, prepared with their axes and finely sharpened machetes, drunk with ambition and the sun.

The first one to come was Don Quinde, accompanied by his wife and three children. He set himself up on Moquiñañas Island. Had brought along some sheets of zinc from his old shanty. And they gave the region its first whitening of zinc. He constructed his house almost as soon as he arrived, living with giant cane, trying to surround himself with as many comforts as possible. Later on, Banchón came. Banchón came alone, the way Don Goyo had come. He raised his house facing Cerrito de los Morreños.

From the very first day, he always appeared with an enormous cigar in his mouth. He carried neither axe nor machete. Nothing but a little knife and a dipping net. The Quindes watched him pass, silent, unsociable, always looking straight ahead. Some months later, the Guayamabe family arrived. And a little later, the Chamaidáns, Captain Lino, the Melgars...

The islands were unable to mount a new defense. And so they surrendered before the assault of this new phalanx. But they surrendered reluctantly, always reserving for Don Goyo their choicest corners, their most intimate secrets. The atmosphere was filled with their cries and noises. There was a prolonged astonishment among the coots and the herons, among the dog fish and the sea bass. Many times they stopped flying or swimming in order to look at what was going on. The pelicans made a gesture of mute protest when they observed the constant encroachment of men. At the beginning they swirled around the intruders. None of the islands' natural inhabitants feared men. But they came to recognize the casting net always spread over the estuary; the agile harpoon always ready to jump; the treacherous hooks holding the bait at the water's surface; and they began to flee. The proximity of the *cholos* was revealed by the emptiness of their surroundings. An oar stroke, or a shout, or a prow cutting the water and sliding over the foam was the signal to disperse.

*   *   *

Almost every week, there arrived in the city log wood and split wood, *mangle* charcoal, a large variety of succulent fish. Many people asked where all these things came from. And then it became known that they came from inside the Chupadores. From some islands that were behind Fort

Punta de Piedra, or farther on, or nearer. They couldn't be quite sure. Some huge islands. Most of them consisting only of salt earth. Although one or another had fertile earth. All were surrounded by thick, greenish black *mangle* groves.

III

At first, Don Goyo withdrew into himself. He felt—just like the islands—deprived of his right to be alone, which he thought he had acquired during the arduous days of his struggle. He did not look at his new neighbors. Kept on living the way he always had. As if nothing had disturbed the peace of earlier days. Many times he encountered them. Sensed that they wanted to talk with him, that they stopped their canoe, that their eyes followed him as if begging. He continued on unperturbed. As if he had seen no one, as if the islands' *mangle* groves were all that mattered to him.

Don Quinde was unable to endure it. One day, in a remote corner of the islands, behind a little hummock of *ñanga* roots, he came upon him.

—Don Goyo!

He was fishing, with the pole and hook stretched over the projections of the branches, trying to catch a few croakers or red snappers. He acted as if he hadn't heard. The other man repeated:

—Don Goyo!

He turned around. Harshly and rudely, he asked:

—What's the matter?

Don Quinde hesitated briefly. Finally, he made up his mind:

—Look, Don Goyo. We've got a keg of "tiger milk."
And we'd like you to have some with us.

—But I don't drink.

—Just a little drink, Don Goyo. It never harmed any
man.

Don Goyo thought it would be ugly to stretch this out
more. Especially on the basis of not drinking.

—All right, then. What time?

—Right now. If that's agreeable.

—It's OK. I'll be there soon. Let me pull in a few monos,
or pompanos, or porgies.

—We'll expect you.

Don Goyo felt enraged. Damn, he had let himself be
caught so easily. It seemed to him that in that moment he was
betraying the islands, that he too should have remained
forever faithful, forever alone, making a world apart. At the
same time, he remembered when he first arrived, how he had
to struggle, how much he suffered from the rough blows of
the strange and hostile environment. And his rage left him
slowly, like the tide receding from a cape's backwaters.

He arrived at Don Quinde's. And met the majority of the
inhabitants of the area. They had waited for him before
downing the first drink. When he climbed up to the cane
house, those present kept absolute silence, staring at him
attentively, minutely, as if he were some rare animal.

—God grant you a good day.

—Good day, Don Goyo.

They immediately brought him one of the empty
kerosene crates so he could sit down. And then they served
him the first drink. This courtesy was paid him by Don
Quinde's wife, a delectable woman with billowing hips.
Don Goyo took his drink in one gulp. And he began—
thoroughly—to look at those around him. He noticed

Captain Lino, who they said was very good at building sloops and caulking canoes. He noticed him particularly because he was a young man, maybe twenty years old.

At first, when they still had drunk nothing, the atmosphere was difficult, oppressive. Conversation died out. Everybody was showing signs of boredom, in spite of the efforts of Don Quinde's wife who fluttered in and out like a fan of lewdness. But later, when the liquor began to ignite their veins and to cloud their minds, the distances became shorter. And everybody commenced to talk, feeling happy to be together for the first time. Especially Don Quinde, who was conversing eagerly with Don Goyo in one corner of the room.

—And you've never become tired of it, Don Goyo?

—Never. Why? I've never lacked for anything. Always had everything I wanted. Why should I grow tired of it?

—But like this, without a woman, all alone?

—No. I've gone to Guayas to look for women. That way you don't have to take care of them or worry about them. Besides, I like being alone. Alone all the time.

—You'll change, Don Goyo, you'll change...

—Anything is possible. But for now...

—For now...

* * *

It was already dark when he headed toward his house. He rowed slowly all the way, looking at the blurred shadow of the *mangles* and thinking about what he had done and said that day. There were moments when he felt that he was beginning a new life. That everything was going to change for him. He sensed a strange premonition in these things. It seemed that an uncommon happiness hung in the air. He felt happy himself, felt his flesh vibrating like rubber.

He thought maybe it was the liquor. The fact was that he had drunk too much. Because it cost him nothing. And even more, he hadn't had a drink for so long. There were also moments when he sensed it was because he had made friends with those people; because from now on he would have someone to speak to, someone to meet during his long canoe trips, and someone to whom he could talk about his struggles and triumphs from time to time. A man—like himself—in the gray whirlwind of the islands! Now it seemed strange to him that he had been able to live alone for so long, that he had been able to hear this obligatory conversation with himself, or with creatures it was so difficult to understand.

He was absolutely convinced. Yes. It was the completion of his happiness. The Quindes, Banchón, the Guayamabes, the Chamaidáns, Captain Lino, the Melgars. All of them danced in his head throughout the night. He felt them suddenly involved in his life. As if he—unexpectedly— had been transformed into an island where a multitude of waving palms had taken root. And—strange indeed—he felt stronger. He saw them gathered all around him. Hanging on to his words and his movements. Astonished that he knew so many things.

* * *

That same night—also—he was aware for the first time of the emptiness of his bed. The deerskin seemed excessively large for him. The cold of the night, too strong. His lust, set on fire, intolerable. And he also came to a conclusion: he needed a wife. A wife who would always sleep with him, especially when he wanted her to. A wife to look after him, who would give him some children, who would always have a meal ready and her legs open and ready for his virile caress.

Thinking about this, he remembered the coming and going of Don Quinde's wife. And his flesh burned hotter and hotter. Once he thought he saw her walking from her house across the estuary like an opulent canoe, completely naked. And that she was calling him, to man her vessel with all the fire of his solitary years.

He was unable to sleep. He spent the whole night getting up, looking at the inlet that seemed to become more and more brilliant, looking at the hazy shadows of the interminable islands that melded into each other in the distance, feeling that a series of strange desires and sensations were crazily urging him on.

* * *

From the next day on, he was everybody's best friend. The *cholos* tacitly granted him tremendous authority over them. They trusted his judgment as definitive. He was a kind of final arbiter. His word was tranformed into law. His advice, a command. They willed him to be a man different from the rest. They granted him all kinds of special considerations. The best seat in every house was always for him. The best coffee and the most flavorful banana. He was clearly accorded a kind of leadership he had never sought, which surrounded him with attention.

He initiated them into the secrets he had discovered during his life on the islands. He helped them fish, cut *mangle*, make charcoal. He always knew where everything was easiest, most productive, and most abundant. Don Quinde, who accompanied him almost all the time, spent many hours talking with him, endeavoring to learn about the rugged life of the islands. And when they were returning home, when they were on their way to rest, rowing slowly, distractedly, drinking in the atmosphere, Don Quinde would unexpectedly speak up:

—Listen, Don Goyo. You ought to get yourself a woman. It's a lot better. This business of doing everything for yourself is very screwed up. There are some things men just can't do.

Don Goyo would laugh and let him talk on.

He too noticed that a wife was becoming a necessity for him. Every day he felt more alone. He realized that suddenly he was going to be old and would have no one, absolutely no one, to take care of him. But at the same time, it pained him to lose his freedom, the freedom to do whatever he wanted to do, the freedom of not having always to cover the same thighs, the same belly that he might grow tired of even after the very first day. It might even happen that the woman would prove to be a bad one who would treat him dirty, and then he would have to put up with it or murder her.

*   *   *

He tried to forget. Knowing that Cerrito de Morreños was fertile land where he could grow anything he planted and spend his time that way, he made a decision. Brought some good seed corn from Guayaquil. And, after clearing the land easily, because there were very few trees and the brush was not heavy, planted his crop.

At the beginning of the winter, there were torrential rains almost every day. It was difficult and dangerous to venture out among *mangles* so slippery that they seemed to have been soaped. To make matters worse, a series of plagues spread much disease. Even Don Goyo was bothered by periodic fevers for several weeks, and he didn't get along very well because there was no one even to boil some water or prepare him a remedy. He had to get out of bed and see what he could find to cure himself. Don Quinde, who visited him on one of his bad days, kept pounding his ears with the same phrases:

—Why don't you get yourself a woman over here, Don Goyo? You see how you're screwed now because nobody will take care of you.

Don Goyo remained silent, but inside, deep down, he knew that Don Quinde was right.

*   *   *

About two months went by. The corn began to produce. The old hill, barren at the summit, was covered now with the slender, spiky plants. A smile of new life polychromed the surroundings. Everything seemed reborn. And Don Goyo felt stronger and stronger, ready to conquer a shark.

IV

That was when he picked out his first wife.

He brought her from Guayas where she was a servant in a White Man's house. He described Cerrito de los Morreños to her as somewhat different from what it was. He offered to provide all she needed, and the luxuries she wanted, and to take her regularly—every week, if possible—to the city. For another thing, he had already made her realize how much a man he was...

That was enough. The woman, whose name was Margarita, made up her mind one fine day and tied up her bundle of clothes. She embarked in Don Goyo's canoe. And she came to Cerrito to live with the lively *cholo*.

It was a constant fiesta. They were coupled together in anguished passion for several days, separating only long enough to eat or to do what was absolutely necessary. They had forgotten the rest of humanity. Several times the neighbors had attempted to visit. But when they distinguished the outline of the writhing couple, they realized that an erotic fever had taken hold of them, and they went away understandingly, mumbling a few ritual phrases. And meanwhile, the untiring couple, now on the deerskin, now on the cane floor, now on the gentle earth or in the canoe, continued their galloping pleasures. Don Goyo had said maliciously that he was making his entrance like nothing less than a real *macho*.

* * *

He inflated Márgara as if she were a balloon. In a few months, she was unable to move. Don Quinde from time to time, would joke with him:

—You've given her four or five babies!

Don Goyo would smile, proudly relishing his fertility and vigor, and he was flattered. Then he would go at it again with Márgara. Don Quinde's wife, when she saw her go by, couldn't hold back a sigh of envy: "If only all men were like Don Goyo! If only Don Quinde didn't get tired so fast!" And sometimes, exalted at the height of her furious passion, she tried to make her husband be copious, abundant. To find strength where it had never existed.

—You ought to learn from Don Goyo. There's a real man for you!

And Don Goyo was becoming stronger. He was walking more resolutely. His paddle was beating the water furiously. A triumphal smile spread over his lips. He realized that he had become a kind of human symbol. And that even the *mangles* along the shore looked at him enviously.

But after their son was born, he forgot Márgara. He even found her repulsive. He didn't want to see her, much less make love to her. The one thing that preoccupied him then was his son. He wanted to be a father just as he had been a husband. Always a model. The best that might be found in the region.

When the child was a few months old, he took charge of him. Don Goyo took him out in the canoe, in spite of his mother's terror. She implored him not to do such a foolish thing. The mosquitos would bite him. He might be burned by too much sun. He might fall overboard. Don Goyo paid no attention. He assured her this was the only way to make a man of him. And that he had been raised that way. On the other hand he also said he would take good care that nothing happened to his son. And Márgara had to resign herself to it.

He took the boy through the thickest *ñanga* tangles. He made him breathe the disagreeable odor of the floating mud. He let the sun's flaming caress pause on the baby's delicate skin. He lay him on the bottom of the canoe so that he could get the feel of the only real hammock. He forced the tiny hands to hold on to the rough, wrinkled handle of the oar. The boy kept hearing his tough advice.

—You have to work hard. In order to learn to be a man, a better man than all the others. In order to lay the women and beat down the men. In order to cut *mangle*. In order to do everything. That's the meaning of Don Goyo around here!

It seemed as if the child understood him. He stared straight at him. And laughed. Laughed listening to the enthusiastic voice of the husky *cholo*.

Over the islands the wind grew stronger and began to rock the canoe. The sky became darker and darker. Great black storm clouds perched atop the *mangles*. It was going to rain any minute.

Don Goyo started home.

*   *   *

When he was bigger and could move around by himself, Don Goyo bought him a small axe and a short-handled machete. Márgara protested again.

—But Don Goyo, the boy will cut his foot or his hand.

—Let him cut it. That way he'll learn not to be clumsy.

And he, with all his faith and enthusiasm, began to teach the boy how to handle his weapons. Under the house, in the shade, he showed him how he should cut the logwood and the stumpwood, and also how to go about peeling the bark of the *mangle*. What the curve is like when one chops a log in the opposite direction. And how to prop one log on another—using it as a kind of pillow—in order to split it. All this, in addition to what the experience acquired during his long years of working had taught him. And at the same time, he made recommendations about the position and intensity with which he ought to work in each case.

He also made him row, and paddle, and fish. The boy's skin toughened fast. Insect bites that at first burned his skin red, now had no effect on him at all. And he was as smiling and as happy beneath the sun that clawed furiously at his shoulders as he was in the water that got colder and colder. Don Goyo, satisfied with his work, murmured over and over:

—I am making him a man.

* * *

When Don Goyo thought his son had finished his apprenticeship and knew enough to help him in everything, he turned again to Márgara. It was another honeymoon. Sexual fever again ignited his veins. He felt stronger than a bull. He plowed his joyful mate in every corner. He pleased her as he had never pleased her before. An expression of happiness appeared on the faces of both husband and wife. The astonished *cholos* began prowling around the place again, hardly believing what they saw. And when they finally did believe it, they couldn't help murmuring:

—That Don Goyo really keeps it up!...

And—naturally—the inevitable happened. Márgara inflated again. Don Goyo avoided her again. And this time they both waited expectantly.

It was a girl. Don Goyo cursed. Protested the treachery of his own flesh and that of his woman. If he had been able he would have thrust the newborn child back into the mother's belly and prohibited its coming out. He neither ate nor helped at the house for several days. It was very hard for him to spend time with that little girl, whom he never wanted, who disgusted him so. And even months later, he still avoided, avoided...

But one evening when he returned from crabbing and was slowly climbing up to the house, he heard a gentle little voice babbling:

—Papa! Papa!

He turned around, startled. And saw the little girl walking toward him. It was like the awakening of a love from a deep sleep. He picked her up. Held her tenderly in his arms. Carried her all through the house. He devoted himself—finally—to his daughter, just as he had devoted himself to his son. Following his monochord system of education, he took her out into the estuaries. This time Márgara made no effort to protest. She let him teach her the same things he had taught the first child: to split wood, to fish, to row, to go crabbing.

* * *

He was definitively reconciled with his wife. He devoted himself completely to her. It was as if he felt a deep urge to plant his seed. Children came one after another in a rosary that seemed interminable. He took time to educate each one. And had them—each one—participate in his good fortune.

Cerrito de los Morreños was transforming itself into a town. Soon the boys themselves became men. Began to look for wives to live with. Had children of their own. Worked for them and for their families. Forming—within their own group—a world apart.

And—unexpectedly—to the disbelief of everyone, Márgara died. She just went away, silent, calm, just as she had lived. Without a word of protest. Without a sign of suffering. They sent her to Guayas, where she had come from. And everyone in the village of Cerrito mourned her.

For some time Don Goyo was disoriented, not knowing what to do. Whatever he undertook, it seemed to him he still had his vigorous mate by his side, the woman who had worked with him so much, who had made his life so lucky and pleasant.

The neighbors and even his own sons advised him to take another wife. But he wanted to be faithful to the memory of Márgara.

* * *

That was when it occurred to him. The best way to forget and to bring his people together was to take on a job they could all participate in. Cutting *mangle*, for example...

Without saying anything to the people of Cerrito, he went to see Captain Lino. And, after explaining his idea, he said:

—Captain, you could build us a small sloop. We will furnish whatever you need. And, if you wish, you can come live in our house. As long as you wish!

To Captain Lino it seemed a good idea. And right away

he headed over to Cerrito. Don Goyo called the whole family together. He explained his plan to them. And the *cholos* agreed to it readily.

Captain Lino went to Guayaquil to get nails, and to get some tool or other that he happened not to have, and some timbers not available around Cerrito. Then he started to work.

—Later on we'll send for the sails and rigging. And we'll buy the anchor and chain.

*   *   *

Everyone who could made his small contribution to the construction of the sloop. Some looked for timbers, others worked them with the axe and the adz. Some planed the surfaces completely smooth.

The first step was to set in place a strong timber, about fifty feet long, to which the frame of the hull was attached. After several days work, the ribbing of the sloop was ready. Then it was necessary to get some money together and buy a few planks to finish the hull.

Next they fastened the mast to the keel, securing it with some crosspieces of the deck. Then they covered part of the deck with planks. The boom came next. And they started some work on the freeboard. They also sent to Guayaquil for the sailcloth and to purchase the anchor and chain.

All this created a number of problems, because they had to find money to buy the different things they needed to finish building the ship.

Finally came the caulking. Captain Lino began by putting coconut palm oakum in all the crevices of the hull. And after forcing it in for a long time, he covered it with boiling pitch, leaving the crevices completely closed. Then he gave the entire hull a tar bath. And finished the freeboard.

*   *   *

The launching of the sloop was a fiesta. Everybody went aboard her. They inched her over the inlet's neck until she fell into the water. She rolled for a few moments. Stirred up a streamer of foam at her prow and then rode calmly, majestically in the middle of the estuary. Captain Lino murmured:

—We'll call her the "Mercedes Orgelina." Nobody dared disagree.

* * *

And that night, that very night, Captain Lino carried off one of Don Goyo's daughters with him. The *cholo* got angry. Wanted to look for him in order to stick a machete in his belly. But he calmed down almost immediately. His old obsession with fertility and fecundity, that had seemed dormant, was coming to life again. He thought of the number of inhabitants his daughter could give to Cerrito. And he pardoned the fugitives. They could come back whenever they wished.

V

He felt stronger than ever. The years seemed to slide over his body, leaving no mark. His muscles were as hard as ever. A longing to live fully constantly excited him. He was the one who worked hardest, and who enjoyed himself most. The people around him were more and more astonished by the old *cholo's* virility and energy. And their respect and love for him grew tumultuously. For them, Don Goyo was a kind of demigod.

They had made a deal with the Electric Company. Every week the "Mercedes Orgelina" hauled log wood. This way they had been able to acquire a few comforts and, even more important, to eat a little better. Now you could hear guitar music and singing almost every evening. And often there was a little liquor to ignite the veins and lighten the heart.

One fine day, Don Goyo said quietly:

—I need another woman!

And—to the astonishment of all—he went to Guayaquil to look for one.

*   *   *

He came back with Ña Andrea, ex-wife of a *montuvio* from the high country who used to beat her every day. Having grown tired of that kind of life, one fine day she had left him and had gone to live in the city. She found work in the house of some Whites. And she stayed there until she met Don Goyo. Although she was getting along in years, Ña Andrea was still a fine female who swayed like a hammock when she walked, lighting an insinuating spark in the eyes of the men who saw her.

She won everybody's friendship almost as soon as she arrived. Her friendly ways, her many kindnesses, and above all her delicious coffee, which no one knew how to prepare as well as she, contributed a great deal to her success. And— more important—because she was Don Goyo's wife, because he had chosen her as first lady and mistress of the islands.

And—once again—the *cholos* were astonished. In spite of being more than a hundred years old, Don Goyo felt more potent than a studhorse. In the night you could hear the straining of his body joined to Na Andrea's. Below their house, they heard him one, two, three, and four times. The following day he would wake up triumphant, joyful, authoritative. And the ample hips of Ña Andrea had the provocative movement of a jumping canoe.

What everyone expected happened again. Ña Andrea inflated. And Ña Andrea had a daughter, Gertru.

She had hardly brought her into the world, after a supreme effort, when she said,

—The first and the last.

She would be on guard. Wished no more children. She would find some way to control that bull of a Don Goyo. Or cast some kind of spell on him. Or find a remedy. She was not going to care for children all her life. She was already an old woman. And anyway. It was too much work...

Over in his corner, Don Goyo laughed mysteriously.

* * *

Several years passed. He felt happier every day. He came to believe that this happiness was eternal. That he would die—when his turn came—happy and peaceful, surrounded by his people, without that devil Tin-Tin patrolling around his house, without ever lacking the necessities of a good christian.

But one day—as ordinary as any other day—someone came to say to him privately:

—You know what's happening, Don Goyo? The Whites are coming. They say they've bought an island. Going to work at different things around here.

He didn't like it much. He had heard many bad things about the Whites. People said that in the high country everything was settled with whips and bullets. And they stole everything the poor *montuvios* had, throwing them off their little farms. Often they even put them in jail. Even more—suddenly—he had a premonition that the Whites would be his undoing.

—Damn them!

Later on, more specific information reached him. About

a White Man named Don Carlos who had come in two sloops, who had bought an island where there was fresh water, who had brought his whole family, who seemed to want to make a business of charcoal and firewood on a large scale, and in addition, to farm the land. Nobody said anything about his background or his plans with respect to them. Somebody reported he had gone to San Miguel del Morro to hire people to help with his work, that he was very rich, that he would arrive in a few days, and that he was tall, blond, and blue-eyed like almost all the Whites.

One fine day the sloops appeared. They passed in front of Cerrito. Kept on into the estuary. They were loaded, heavy sterned, full of people who leaned over the gunwales to stare at the *cholos'* houses. They were big ships, very big. They sailed majestically and proudly toward the gray labyrinth of enormous islands.

The same day a canoe with new people arrived at Cerrito. A man jumped out amidst the barking of the dogs.

—Fine day!

—Fine!

Don Goyo went down to welcome them:

—Come up! Come up!

The tide was high. The water came up to the stanchions of the house. The sun made the surroundings boil like a kettle.

—We came over here to ...

—Go on ...

—Don Carlos sends his respects and wants you to go talk with him. He wants to see if you will deal ...

He had doubts. Why didn't he come to see him himself, if we wanted to talk? Did he look down on Don Goyo? Maybe because he was not a White? Then it occurred to him, probably because the old man was so generous, that the White Man was tired, and so had not come to see him, but had sent for him to come. And anyway, he had nothing to lose. So...

—All right.

* * *

The following day he got up very early. Set out in his canoe. And slowly headed toward Don Carlos' place.

As soon as he arrived, the White Man came down to the shore. They stood looking at each other briefly. Don Goyo murmured:

—Good day, Don Carlos.

—Good day, Don Goyo.

He jumped out. The White Man slapped him on the back and shook his hand.

—How are you?

—Well, not bad, Don Carlos. And you?

—Just fine, Don Goyo.

He took him up to the house, which was partially built, well enough for the first few days. He offered a drink. And he said:

—Look, Don Goyo. I sent for you in order to tell you I've come to these islands to work with all of you. What I want to do is improve all this. But I don't want it all for me; I want it to be a common property. You understand? That's why I need the help of your people. You yourself can help me with them. And you can teach me something about the life of these islands, which I know hardly anything about. We can work together. For the good of everybody.

—All right.

He liked the idea. It was one of his dreams. To transform his surroundings completely. To make them into a center of great activity and production, with men and canoes coming and going, as in Guayas. The only problem was that he doubted the words of the White Man. It all sounded like a lie to him, that the one thing being attempted was to trap and persuade the *cholos* to work for the White Man's benefit, that he would leave the islands no better off than they had been before, maybe even using a whip in dealing with the natives, like the White's in the high country.

But then he thought that it was even worse to doubt this way, from the beginning, without having any real reason for his doubts. It was better to wait. To let things run their course. And in the end he would see what it was that he had to do.

—All right, Don Carlos.

Another slap on the shoulder. Another shot of liquor. And then, the farewell.

—All right, Don Carlos.

*   *   *

That's the way it was. That same day, he called his people together in Cerrito. He told them about Don Carlos' projects, explaining to them the reported advantages of this new form of work. The *cholos* agreed, and resolved to cooperate with the White Man in any way possible.

A great number of them went to work as peons. They were earning one *sucre* and sixty *centavos* an hour. They moved, with their wives, thinking they were going to enjoy the best period of their lives. Others agreed to deliver wood in their canoes, and to take their pay partly in food supplies and partly in money. But always continuing to live in Cerrito.

At the beginning, everything went well. They earned their first week's pay. There was a lot of movement on the estuary. In the most distant parts of the archipelago, there was talk about the gigantic project that Don Carlos had undertaken, and that you could take anything over there and sell it. But later on, the ones who were working as peons began to notice that what they were earning didn't amount to anything, that it was all going for food, and even worse, that their debts were piling up. As soon as they were sure about what was happening, they told Don Goyo about it. He listened to them without saying a single word.

Some days later, Don Quinde presented himself in Cerrito. The *cholo* was obviously nervous, wondering whether he should speak or not. He approached Don Goyo in a confidential manner.

—Listen, Don Goyo.

—What is it, Don Quinde?

—Well, it seems that...

—Go ahead and tell it, Don Quinde.

—Well, you see, Don Goyo... The other day Don Carlos came to my house. He was there almost all the evening and he started pumping me... About whether I knew you or not, about how many years you've lived in these parts, about who was the owner of Cerrito and whether he had any papers to prove it, about how much he liked it, about how he hadn't taken it away from you because you're an old man. And about how, as soon as you die...

—I see.

He had listened without saying a word, calmly, without letting even the slightest movement of his body reveal the tempest within.

—All right... Many thanks, Don Quinde.

* * *

He knew enough. He called his people together one Sunday. Told them he could see that working for the White Man was not turning out to be a good thing, that it would be better for them to keep on sending wood to Guayaquil on their own. Because the way things were going, the "Mercedes Orgelina," standing idle, would just rot, after they had

worked so hard to build her. Besides, it was time now for
them to create a new, independent life.

The *cholos* obeyed him once more, as they always had.

Of course, they would continue to be friends with Don
Carlos. They would help him any way they could. But they
would not work for him anymore. That wouldn't do.
Besides, he had had a secret premonition that seemed about
ready to be fulfilled...

*   *   *

Another handful of years passed. Everything went back
to normal. Don Carlos seemed to forget that Don Goyo,
Cerrito de los Morreños, and the *cholo* settlement existed.
His project continued even more successfully. And whenever
the two men met by chance, they always greeted each other
cordially.

—How are you, Don Carlos?

—How are you, Don Goyo?

If there was a fiesta in one place or another, Don Carlos
and Don Goyo were always the first ones invited.

*   *   *

Then came that fatal day of the wake, after which
everything had changed, and finally came the denial of his
authority that had just happened.

—Damn it all!

VI

Don Goyo had remembered all this without interrup-
tion. And he had felt it and seen it, as if he were living it
again.

It was beginning to grow dark. The lamps flickered timidly in the corners of the house. The inlet seemed to start a furious gallop toward the distant horizons. The *mangles* intertwined their branches. All the surroundings were filled with a majestic, imposing silence.

Don Goyo left the window. With a hesitant gait, he went down the steps. He walked toward the shore. And boarded his canoe. The *cholos*, motionless, astonished, followed his every movement, watching him until he disappeared in the intricate labyrinth of the estuaries.

Don Leitón said hoarsely:

—I think it's bad, what Don Goyo's doing!

*   *   *

Don Goyo rowed slowly, as if sleep were gradually overtaking him. His canoe followed the whim of the currents, making unexpected movements.

Night was coming on fast. Everything was coming together in the archipelago. The cold was sharpening its slender harpoons in order to drive them into the skin of men and of things. Again you could hear the voice of the islands' inhabitants.

Unexpectedly, Don Goyo had the sensation of growing old. It seemed that all at once he had lost his vigor and his youthful strength. His muscles grew slack and his skin wrinkled. He saw nothing. Heard nothing. All his senses had suddenly atrophied. A strange dance of absurd images took place in his primitive mind.

He saw first that the canoe was rearing up. Jumping fantastically over the mobile skin of the inlet. It carried him almost flying toward the shore, as if it were trying to crash into the *mangles*. His efforts to control it were useless, absolutely useless.

Seized by a strange fear, he threw himself into the water.

Commenced to swim, to swim as well as he was able, feeling
his strength failing him all the while. And it seemed that the
canoe was following him, still rearing up. Now it was almost
up with him. The bow was nearly touching him. Then he
saw his arms like a whirlpool. He was flying, not swimming.
It seemed that the water was just grazing him gently. And
he—master over all—was stirring up foam like a great shark.

He reached shore almost immediately. It seemed that the
canoe was down at the foot of the *mangles,* waiting for him,
trying—vainly—to climb up through the mud. Don Goyo
laughed. A savage, brutal laugh that no one had ever heard.

It seemed that the *mangles* were beginning to move.
Waving their enormous, knotty limbs, like monstruous gray
serpents, trying to trap him.

He ran. He jumped over the ribs of the slippery roots.
Several times he fell—he who had never fallen before. He cut
his skin on the sharp oyster shells. Little by little, the feeling
grew that snails and spiders were climbing over his body. A
swarm of mosquitos covered him like a black sheet. Among
the projecting *ñangas,* he could see the wizard shrimp, the
sin bocas, the "conchcrackers," and the crabs that seemed to
be following him. And the *mangles*—more terrifying by the
minute—seemed to amuse themselves grinding their huge
branches near the ears of Don Goyo.

*   *   *

He was bleeding. Bleeding in a thousand places. His
flesh had become an absurd mass of pain. Faint, exhausted,
he dragged himself along, holding on with his nails, with
his teeth, with his whole body; sometimes in the mud, or over
the roots; once in a while among the high and hostile
branches. He was losing awareness of his surroundings.
Everything in his mind was becoming hazy and he could no

longer feel the pain from the slashes of the oyster shells, the biting of the insects, or the blows of the agitated roots.

Unexpectedly he started to experience a certain tranquility and sweetness. Believed he saw the *mangles* gradually coming toward him. Believed that they were reaching out their powerful limbs to caress him. And then he felt the branches lift him gently, transporting him across all the islands.

His progress was greeted with indications of respect. A whispering of admiration and affection boiled up in the remotest corners, in the muddy coves. And it seemed that a great multitude of *mangles* began to follow the ones that carried the old *cholo* in their branches.

Don Goyo was happy.

VII

Very early—when it was still dark—they went out to cut *mangle*. They were happy. With a lightheartedness that was apparent in their smiles. They rowed furiously, driving the paddle with a force that had been absent for a while. Their canoes cut through the water like rays in heat. Everybody was talking about the behavior of Don Goyo.

—Looks like Don Goyo got pretty mad.

—He'll get over it.

—I don't know why, but I'm worried about him.

—Don't be a fool! What could happen to Don Goyo? And besides, we were screwing ourselves just to please him!

—That's true.

The axes seemed to be listening in the bottom of the canoe. The smoke of the termite nest, lit to drive away the insects, went out gradually, over in its corner, completely forgotten by the *cholos*. Dawn fled over the greenish black hump of the islands.

*　*　*

They stopped not far from home.
—Let's not waste time going in far. We need to cut a lot as soon as we can so we can go sell it to the White Man.
—Yeah.
They jumped out. Tied their canoes to a firmly driven stake. Picked up their axes, and half buried themselves in the thick network of the palms.
Almost immediately, the blow of an ax rang out. A strange blow that seemed to resound, hostile, over all the islands. And then, yes. A kind of scream emerged from every slashed *mangle*. They felt rocked in rage. The moving earth trembled in waves of anguish. A strange sound of protest seemed to swell in the atmosphere.
—There's something happening that I don't like.
—You're crazy! It's all in your head. Stop loafing!
—And what if Tin-Tin is out to screw us? We'll really be in a mess.
—Go on, cut some wood. And stop talking bullshit.
The trunks started falling, crushing hundreds of smaller ones as they fell. It looked as if the high limbs were flailing, trying to grab on to others. Or to balance themselves and stay upright. Then—giving up—they fell thunderously, their weaker parts breaking to bits.

*　*　*

The *cholos* began trimming them. Quickly they climbed up on the fallen trunks and stripped off their branches with short, well-aimed axe strokes. Once the trunk was left perfectly clean, they began to cut it into more or less uniform pieces, and stacked them. When they were all cut and stacked, they started loading them on the canoes.

—Now we'll carry this to the White Man.

—I think the White Man always makes fools of us.

—He's the only one who can help us.

—Damn it all!

In spite of it all, they did not feel completely happy. They started toward Don Carlos' place rowing sluggishly, slowly, unenthusiastically, as if they wished never to arrive.

—It feels like we're going backwards!

This statement, the way it was said, unexpectedly and somewhat sarcastically, revived them a little. And the paddle began to beat on the inlet's rippling surface with more authority.

* * *

They arrived at Don Carlos' place. Unloaded the wood in front of his house. Worked in the mud much of the time because the tide was low. After a while there was a stack of wood, and the canoes were empty. The dogs barked all the time, but since the *cholos* had worked there, they didn't bite them, or even come very near.

—Good day, Don Carlos.

—Good day.

After a while, the White Man came out.

—What do you want?

—Well, nothing, White Man; we just brought this wood to see if you want it.

Don Carlos looked annoyed. He put his hand to his head. He scratched several times. Finally he muttered:

—But man! I don't want any wood. I have all I can use.

In Guayaquil they don't even want to buy it. And when they do buy it, they don't pay enough to cover the cost of shipping it. Sorry...but I don't want any more wood. Sell it to somebody else. To Don Quinde, for example. He takes wood to Guayaquil too.

The *cholos* began to whisper among themselves. Don Carlos pretended not to notice. Don Leitón murmured:

—The White Man is going to fuck us. Everything he's said is a lie. What he wants is for us to sell him the wood cheap. And what are we going to do? We'll have to let him have it.

And turning to Don Carlos, he said:

—Look, Don Carlos, we'll let you have it cheap.

—No, man, not even as a gift. What am I going to do with all that wood?

—No matter how much there is, if you sell it at half price, there'll always be somebody to buy it.

Don Carlos looked bored.

—All right, then...

*   *   *

They went back to Cerrito. Went back sullen, almost without talking. The White Man had taken advantage of them in every way. Not only in the price of the wood, but also in the price and the measure of the food supplies that he had sold them.

When they arrived, Ña Andrea came down. She ran toward the canoe and asked:

—Did you see Don Goyo anywhere?

—No, Ña Andrea. Why?

—Because I haven't seen him since last night. He didn't sleep here and he didn't say anything to anybody.

—That's bad. We'll wait for him. Maybe he's out

hunting in the bush. Or out fishing to teach us a lesson. Because last night we told him we didn't want to fish anymore.

—That could be. But my heart is jumping.

They went up to their houses. Made their wives—those who had wives—delouse them. And went to sleep.

The sun made the whole archipelago boil silently. It came in great burning waves that scorched the blood of the men and the sap of the trees. And it plunged into the inlet, spiking it.

* * *

Don Leitón arose at noon. Everybody around him was snoring. Ña Andrea was sitting alone by the window, watching the inlet.

—What's wrong, Ña Andrea? Isn't Don Goyo back yet?

—No. Not a sign of him. I think something bad has happened. The "stake bird" cried the whole night long.

—Don't believe it, Ña Andrea. We'll wait for him until it grows dark; and if he doesn't come, we'll go look for him.

—Good.

Don Leitón couldn't go back to sleep. He too was beginning to feel uneasy. He remembered that Don Goyo had never before let so much time pass without coming home.... And when he had to be late, for one reason or another, he had always sent word. Something had happened to the old *cholo*.

Don Leitón began to feel a kind of remorse for what he had said to Don Goyo. And thinking about it more, maybe the old man's idea was right. Maybe it would have been better to fish. That very morning he had seen how the White Man had taken advantage of them.

* * *

By nightfall, everybody was awake. Don Goyo had still not appeared. Ña Andrea was becoming more and more upset. Nobody had fixed anything to eat or bothered about anything else. All of them were anxiously looking toward the horizon, trying to see whether the black dot had appeared that would indicate the presence of a canoe. Don Leitón began to conjecture about where Don Goyo might have been, and what he might have gone to do. And then he divided the *cholos* into several groups so each could go exploring independently in a canoe.

He urged Ña Andrea not to worry. Assured her they would find Don Goyo, if anything had happened to him. And that from now on, they would do what he wanted them to do: Fish. Or crab, whatever he said. And that if nothing had happened to him, he would come to Cerrito by himself, on his own. But all his efforts to calm her were in vain. She listened to him silently, unbelieving, soaking up the estuary with her eyes.

* * *

The evening was filling up with shades of gray. The wind was dying down gradually. The *mangle* leaves and the inlet waters became motionless. There was not the slightest noise. All was silent, melancholy. Even the *cholos* were afraid to talk.

The groups set out in their respective canoes. And they rapidly pulled away from shore. Ña Andrea and the other women stood watching them a long time, until they saw them disappear among the low hills suggested by the islands' curving surface.

VIII

As they scattered among the inlets, the first thing each group did was to begin to shout as loud as possible:

—Don Goyooooo!

But they heard only the multiple echo:

—Goyoooooooo!

Anxiously, their eyes pierced the intricate net of vegetation like two question marks. There was no trace of anything human. The search became more and more monotonous and irritating. Some rowed slowly, dipping their paddles unhurriedly, letting the canoe almost follow the rhythm of the current. And from time to time, they would call out again:

—Hey, Don Goyooooo!

And the multiple voice of the echo answered again, as always:

—Goyoooooooo!

* * *

Night was coming on. The rows of *mangle* disappeared in the shadow. The men began to confuse themselves with their surroundings. Gradually they had grown tired of shouting, and now they began to talk quietly among themselves.

—Hell! It looks like the water has swallowed him!

—I don't believe it ... Don Goyo would float even if he tried to drown. One evening I saw him sleeping on the water, just like he was sleeping in a hammock.

—Maybe so. but he's not showing up anywhere, and that's bad.

—He might have gotten really mad about what we said to him, and could be holed up in any of these houses around here. He may even have gone to Guayas.

—He's capable of it!

They continued calling him. Their shouts were weaker. And they resounded strangely over the gray musical staff of the islands.

—Hey, Don Goyo!

—Goyoooo!

They felt afraid. A deep and absurd fear that climbed up in their throats like a clinging vine. Silently they absorbed all the quiet of the archipelago. Pierced the harpoon of their anguish into the funereal slab of black night.

*   *   *

Unexpectedly, a strange tremor moved over the quivering skin of the inlet. They heard a distant roar. After that, a frightful, overwhelming noise, as if all the islands were sinking. It lasted only a few seconds. They heard a noise like the breaking of huge limbs and an infinite rustling of leaves. And, almost immediately, silence. An enormous silence more violent than an explosion.

The *cholos* were quiet for a half an hour or more. They had stopped rowing. They were letting the current carry them along. Exploring—never stopping that, of course—the most tangled recesses in the twisting course of the estuary.

Finally Don Leitón decided to speak:

—Something is happening here tonight. I've been feeling like somebody had taken hold of me by my hair. And I've been afraid. In spite of the fact that I'm really not afraid of anybody.

—That's true.

—Could it have been a big tree falling? Or maybe one of the islands sank. They say that happened here once.

—It could be!

—My head's still spinning. Damn it!

* * *

They rowed all night and in every direction, examined the last mound of *mangles* and the most distant and difficult *ñanga* tangle. Their search produced nothing. It seemed that Don Goyo had in fact been swallowed up by the estuary.

It was almost dawn, when they were so worn out they couldn't go on, after laboring day and night, that Don Leitón—without really believing it—proposed:

—Let's go back. Maybe he's gotten back to Cerrito.

—Let's go back!

Slowly they returned. They were half-conscious, once in a while putting paddle to water, silent, downcast.

Ña Andrea was waiting for them on shore.

—Has he come back?

—No. Did you find anything?

—Not a sign. The man has disappeared like smoke.

They went up to the houses. Everybody was awake. As soon as they arrived, the women gathered around, besieging them with questions. Finally, Don Leitón, annoyed, muttered:

—All right, stop pestering us. Give us a cup of coffee to warm us up and take away the sleepiness that's doubling us over.

They sat on the rough cane floor, on *petate* mats or deerskins, on crates or trunks. And they settled down to wait. They weren't going to sleep. What good would that do?

Dawn was beginning to fade the pure black of the sky,

especially over the humps of the islands. They distantly heard the awakening of all the *mangle* groves. The current of the estuary, running over the *ñangas*, growled softly.

* * *

When it was completely light and they had drunk their coffee, Don Leitón was the first to stand up.

—All right, let's see if we can find Don Goyo now. We can't work today unless we find the Old Man!

They all spoke:

—That's right.

And they boarded their canoes again.

Drowsiness attacked them furiously, in spite of the coffee and the morning light. It was as if a million ants were crawling slowly over their bodies, making them tingle. It seemed that the objects they saw were gradually becoming vaguer and grayer. They hardly knew what they were doing.

Unexpectedly, Cusumbo's voice rang out:

—Don Goyo's canoe!

It was adrift, unoccupied, without direction, swept along by the current. The paddle was in it, on the bottom. It was half full of water. Moving very rapidly.

The *cholos* immediately pulled up to it.

—This business is looking ugly now. Don Goyo has thrown himself into the water!

—What could have happened to him?

—Maybe he drowned.

—And if he drowned, it was because he wanted to. No water in the world could master him.

Two of them boarded Don Goyo's canoe and started rowing. Quickly the two boats picked up speed. Now the *cholos'* fatigue and sleepiness were completely gone. They rowed furiously, as if someone were chasing them.

Don Leitón suggested:

—Keep looking down in the water, boys. If he's drowned, he must be floating. Unless he's hung up in a *ñanga*.

—All right.

* * *

As they rounded a hummock near Pozudo, they saw that the oldest *mangle* on the islands had fallen across the inlet. Its gigantic limbs were sunk into the water. Its roots, torn apart, broken, bleeding, were sticking out of the mud, as if to march away. The dull muttering of the dammed up current ululated around them. Little eddys formed as the water flowed across the fallen timbers.

—What we heard last night...

—Right.

They approached rapidly, impelled by a secret foreboding. Penetrated into the mass of half-fallen foliage bordering the enormous, titanic trunk, venerable in its monstrosity and strength.

Then suddenly, with an indescribable tone, crazy with rage and grief that made them tremble, they heard the voice of Don Leitón:

—God damn!

Astonished, ecstatic, they turned toward him.

—What!...

—Don Goyo!

He didn't have to show them. They found him instantly.

He was submerged in the water, absolutely naked, hanging from one of the strongest branches of the fallen *mangle*. His eyes were open, and his mouth was illuminated by an expression of laughter that was majestic. His muscles had swollen. The body created an impression of strength and exuberance. Dark, wrinkled, strong, it seemed to become one with the flesh of this colossal inhabitant of the islands.

—Don Goyo!

They were afraid to approach him. It seemed to them that the old *cholo* was going to move and speak to them. That he might catch hold of them and drag them to the bottom of the inlet, to sleep the best of all sleeps among the fish and the shells.

—Don Goyo!

Don Leitón, at last, made up his mind. He caught him by his hair, submerging his arm a little. When he had him afloat, the others helped him, trembling. They lifted him up and laid him on the floor of the canoe.

They began to row slowly, feeling that their flesh was swaying like hammocks and their teeth were trying to jump out.

—Don Goyo!

IX

Ña Andrea, having scarcely seen him, murmured:

—We have to send him to San Miguel!

She wept not a tear. Uttered no word of grief or of protest. She retreated to one of the corners of the house and stared empty-eyed at the scene that was taking place around her. Anybody looking at her would have thought she was a stranger among mourners she had come upon by chance.

Don Leitón expanded on what Ña Andrea had said.

—Yes, we have to send him right away, before he swells up even more or maybe bursts. Let's prepare the biggest canoe right away. I need two oarsmen.

Captain Lino rapidly constructed a coffin, roughly finished, with the first boards he could find. They placed Don Goyo in it, partially wrapped in sheets. After that, they took him to the canoe. The *cholos* boarded. And commenced to row.

Ña Andrea commented:

—We couldn't even hold a wake for him!

* * *

The day went by, monotonous, boring. All the *cholos* sat around in their corners, not knowing what to do or say. No one bothered to eat or do anything. At the very most, they took a siesta, hoping to quiet the uneasiness of their spirit.

And the fact is it seemed to them that—after all—they alone were to be blamed for the old *cholo's* death, because they had not listened to him when he probably was right, as always. At times they imagined the old *cholo's* battle with himself, wondering whether or not he should abandon his wife, his children, his people, and especially his Cerrito.

From time to time, one of them would go to the window and stare at the endless water that kept moving on interminably, as if it had done nothing.

* * *

After night had come, Cusumbo invited Gertru to go down to the shore. The *chola* had lost all will of her own and would follow him anywhere.

—All right, let's go!

They sat down on some huge limbs that reached almost into the water. They sat glued together, always aware of their sexual attraction for each other. They talked quietly, gently, feeling that the words were twisting in their throats and were difficult to say.

The night was dark. There was an irritating wind that stirred up everything around them. A din of intermittent noises kept striking their ears. Only the houses of Cerrito de los Morreños remained silent and melancholy.

Cusumbo lamented the death of Don Goyo.

—It's a fact, Gertru. He was the best man I've ever known! And what a man! ... Imagine! He's your father, and still his great-great-grandchildren seem like your brothers and sisters.

—That's true!

—And look what has happened because we wanted to cut *mangle.*

—We had to live. And a man has to make a living anyway he can, with God's help!

—Maybe so. But it still hurts me.

—And who doesn't it hurt?

Cusumbo had begun to place his arm behind her back, and had gently but firmly begun to pull her toward his body. She initiated a movement of protest.

—You're starting that again ...

—Well ...

He was unable to finish. Gertru murmured anxiously:

—Look!

There, in the middle of the river, was Don Goyo. He seemed to be slapping at the blackness of the night. He was sliding over the water as if he were on solid ground. His strength seemed greater than ever before. All around him were hammerheads and tiger sharks that appeared to follow him submissively, weaving carpets of foam as he moved. He was absolutely naked. Was laughing a strange, triumphant laugh.

He stood looking at them briefly. Raised his right hand. Made a fleeting gesture of farewell and started swimming.

He moved slowly, with an impressive dignity. Behind him—in a school—the dark bodies of the sea monsters.

Cusumbo stammered:

—Are we dreaming while we're awake?

—Maybe so... We haven't been asleep.

—Anyway, we'll get married next week.

—Good.

The vision didn't last long. Suddenly they heard the noise of a whirlwind. They saw Don Goyo jump, an unbelieveable jump. The waves of leaping waters broke against the shore. Then everything disappeared in the shadows of black night...

* * *

Several hours later—when everyone was asleep on their deerskins, under insect nets—the dogs started barking. Ña Andrea was the first to get up and go to the window.

—Who is it?

Don Leitón's voice, heavy with emotion, came up from the shore:

—It's me, Ña Andrea!

As soon has she heard him, she went down the hill, almost flying. In a second, she was beside the newcomers.

—What's happened to you, Don Leitón?

—Well, I'll tell you, Ña Andrea... some bad luck... Something I can't explain.

And with a tone half sorrowful, half fearful, he began to narrate...

All day things had gone well for them. The dead man had caused them no trouble at all. Maybe a little odor... but that was natural. They had gotten as far as Cascajal, but couldn't cross because it was too stormy. So they had to wait for nightfall.

It was obviously hard for the old *cholo* to continue talking. He was beginning to tremble. His voice kept breaking. His sentences came hard. However, making an effort, he continued:

—We made the passage at Cascajal very late. It had calmed a little. I told the boys to row hard so we would get there soon, before the body started decomposing. And that's what we were doing when, suddenly, we felt everything tremble and heard a splashing noise. We looked around and then all our flesh turned water, swaying like hammocks of fear. Don Goyo had disappeared, coffin and all. We searched for him a while. But who could find a dead man in Cascajal, and at night! Tomorrow we'll go look for him, if you want us to.

Ña Andrea stood looking at him closely, for a long time. She spoke as if to herself:

—No, Don Leitón. Let's not look for him any more. What good would it do? . . . It all had to be this way!

TRANSLATORS' AFTERWORD

Don Goyo was first published—in Spanish, of course—in 1933. The most widely recognized Spanish-American novels of the time dealt with the Indian problem, as in Jorge Icaza's *Huasipungo,* or with some regional peculiarity that made Spanish America seem exotic to outsiders—the struggle between progress and obscurantism in Rómulo Gallegos' *Doña Bárbara,* for example.

For the most part, these denunciatory novels were cast in a realistic mold that leaves little or nothing to the readers' imagination. But there were also novels of an entirely different kind, like María Luisa Bombal's *La última niebla (The Final Mist),* a story of a woman and her fantasized lover, or like Juan Filloy's *Op Oloop,* an account of the main character's personality disintegration. These novels, and others like them, use innovative narrative techniques to carry their message; they frequently border on the unreal, or even cross over into that undefined territory.

Don Goyo has characteristics of both lines of fiction; it denounces the destruction of a subculture, the *cholo* island people in the Gulf of Guayaquil, but the novel is far from a photographic representation. In fact, it is based on a melding of reality with a factor of unreality that is essential to our appreciation of Don Goyo and his people.

This combination of social concern and innovative perception is characteristic also of a Cuban novel published the same year as *Don Goyo*—Alejo Carpentier's voodoo story, *Ecue-Yamba-O.* The folkloric magic—or magic folklore—of these books appears in a number of later

Spanish-American novels, by the same authors and also by such other writers as Miguel Angel Asturias and Gabriel Garcîa-Márquez.

Demetrio Aguilera-Malta was born in 1909. He was introduced to the *cholo* culture when, as a boy, he visited the island area with older members of his family. Later he belonged to a group of socially committed writers known as the "Grupo de Guayaquil." Along with two of its members, he published a volume of short stories in 1930. Each of Aguilera-Malta's stories bears a title beginning "The *cholo* who...". The most famous of them, "The *cholo* who took revenge," written when the author was eighteen years old, reveals the main stylistic traits that are essential in *Don Goyo*, his first novel. Dialog tends to be flat, uninformative; emotional impact is created by the narrator's highly suggestive description of the natural surroundings.

Aguilera-Malta's perception of the *cholo* and his world is basically poetic. The narrative *about* this world, in *Don Goyo*, tends to be lyrical—imagistic and rhythmic. When the characters speak, however, they do so in a very simple manner. This procedure avoids the portrayal of a falsely poetic *cholo*, while at the same time infusing his characterization with the poetic essence that the novelist sensed in his island friends. It is interesting to note that, in his early work, Aguilera-Malta wrote an approximate phonetic transcription of his characters' speech. He abandoned this practice after the first edition of *Don Goyo*— happily so, from the standpoint of the translator, who faces enough problems without the burden of regional phonetics.

A satisfying reading of the novel may stem from the following contrasting associations: on the one hand, poetic narration-cultural essence-Don Goyo-irreality; on the other hand, simplistic dialog-daily living-Cusumbo-reality. Cusumbo is the commonplace embodiment of the culture; Don Goyo is its legend. There is a time in the course of the novel when Don Goyo is a flesh-and-blood human, but even then he is a hero. Later, he becomes a part of Nature. To a considerable extent, this contrast and the development of Don Goyo are made apparent by the very structure of the novel. Therefore, the transition into English creates no special problem. Specific references that contribute detailed effects to the ambience are a different matter: the names of various fish, bivalves, swampland plants, and the like. In the present translation, some of these things are translated into English equivalents, some are left in Spanish, others are given in literal English translations even though there may be no corresponding English name. The story deals with a relatively isolated people with two possible means of livelihood and with relatively untechnologized customs. The translation assumes such a community—an island of fishermen—and makes the linguistic factor as English as possible.

After Don Goyo, Aguilera-Malta wrote a similar novel, *La isla virgen (The Virgin Island)*, and the highly denunciatory *Canal Zone*. Following a stay in Spain and a book about the Spanish civil war, he spent a number of years writing for the theatre and making films. He wrote three historical novels, and in the late nineteen-sixties returned definitively to the novel with *Seven Moons/Seven Serpents*, a book in which the magic folklore, so important in *Don Goyo*, comes to full fruition. *El secuestro del general (The General's Been Kidnapped!)* is a bitingly humorous political satire. In *Jaguar*, the novelist again focuses on magic folklore and, in *Requiem for the Devil*, he expresses his deeply human yearning for a world without racism.

Aguilera-Malta is an astoundingly creative man. While moving about among stories, poetry, novels, plays, and films, he has also been involved in diplomacy and in education. Most recently he has returned to an early love—painting.

ABOUT THE AUTHOR...

Demetrio Aguilera-Malta, the legendary Ecuadorean writer who until recently has been largely unknown in the English-speaking world, is widely acknowledged to be one of the brilliant pioneers of magic realism, the phantasmagorical style that uniquely characterizes so much of contemporary Latin-American literature. *Don Goyo,* his first novel, was published nearly half a century ago, and is now well-recognized as a classic and utterly timeless work.

In his rich and varied career as a writer, Aguilera-Malta has been a foreign correspondent, has written and directed films, has taught in several universities, and today actively pursues his longstanding love of painting, as well as continuing to write novels of astonishing power and radical inventiveness. He is currently his country's Ambassador to Mexico.